I'm a hustler now, is that it?"

Too caught up in her own fury, Larkin missed the gathering tension. "I don't know, are you? Kind of funny how things changed. One minute, you're just some guy flirting. Then you see me with my father, the futures trader, and suddenly you go all continental on me, with the hand kissing and the heavy stares and…" She swallowed, remembering the flare of heat and need, noticing for the first time the palpable tension that hung around him.

"And?" Christopher bit off, a dangerous flash in his eyes.

She flushed. "And nothing. If you're going to try to get alongside my father through me, you're going to have to do a lot more to convince me than just kiss my hand."

"Gladly." And before she knew what he was about, he'd dragged her to him, lips coming down hot and possessive on hers.

Dear Reader,

The hardest part of finishing a book is saying goodbye to the characters. That was nowhere as true as when I finished *Under His Spell,* the last book in HOLIDAY HEARTS, and had to say goodbye to the Trask family. Imagine how thrilled I was when my editor invited me to bring them back one more time as part of the Famous Families promotion to celebrate Harlequin's sixtieth anniversary. I loved spending time with all the characters again, finding out what's happened in their lives since the last book ended. The best part is that there are a few more Trask cousins where this one came from, so who knows—maybe we'll see the family back again, by popular demand.

I'd love to hear what you think of the story, so drop me a line at Kristin@kristinhardy.com. And don't forget to watch for the rest of THE McBAINS OF GRACE HARBOR series, coming in 2010. In the meantime, stop by www.kristinhardy.com for news, recipes and contests, or to sign up for my newsletter to be informed of new releases.

Enjoy!

Kristin Hardy

KRISTIN HARDY
Always Valentine's Day

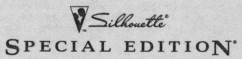

SPECIAL EDITION

Published by Silhouette Books

America's Publisher of Contemporary Romance

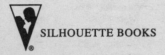 SILHOUETTE BOOKS

ISBN-13: 978-0-373-65434-5
ISBN-10:   0-373-65434-0

Recycling programs for this product may not exist in your area.

ALWAYS VALENTINE'S DAY

Visit Silhouette Books at www.eHarlequin.com

Printed in U.S.A.

KRISTIN HARDY

has always wanted to write, and started her first novel while still in grade school. Although she became a laser engineer by training, she never gave up her dream of being an author. In 2002, her first completed manuscript, *My Sexiest Mistake*, debuted in Harlequin's Blaze line; it was subsequently made into a movie by the Oxygen network. Kristin lives in New Hampshire with her husband and collaborator. Check out her Web site at www.kristinhardy.com.

To the usual suspects for doing what they usually do
(you know who you are),
to Least Goat, for daring to dream,
to Harlequin, for giving us
happily ever after for 60 years,
and to Stephen, for giving me
happily ever after for eleven years.
And counting.

Acknowledgments

Thanks go to Laini Fondiller of Lazy Lady Farm,
and Kristan Doolan and Layla Masant
of Doe's Leap Farm (www.vtcheese.com)
for teaching me about goat dairying,
and to Andy and Jenny Tapper of Via Lactea Farm
(www.vialacteafarm.com) for introducing me to their
goats and showing me what life on a working farm is like.

Chapter One

Larkin Hayes looked across the glassed-in lido deck of the *Alaskan Voyager* to Vancouver Bay beyond. When she'd left L.A. that morning, the mercury had been headed for the mid-nineties. Here in Vancouver, it hadn't even cracked sixty degrees.

A snatch of the *Lost* theme song had her pulling her BlackBerry from her pocket.

"Hello?"

"I'm just leaving the airport," a voice said without preamble.

Five years might have passed since she and her father had spoken regularly, but Carter Hayes seemed to have no doubt that she'd recognize his voice.

And she did. She just couldn't believe what he was saying. "You're only now leaving the airport?"

"My flight got delayed in Tokyo."

"You're aware the ship sails in a little over half an hour, right? We've already done the lifeboat drill."

"I think I can find a lifeboat on my own."

"The question is whether you're going to be able to find the ship in time." Then again, Carter had always been able to do just about anything he wanted—except maybe make a marriage last.

"They won't sail without me," he said confidently.

"If you're lucky."

"I'll be lucky."

One corner of her mouth tugged up. Quintessentially Carter. What wasn't quintessentially Carter was booking fare on a commercial cruise line for their trip. He could have chartered a yacht; hell, he probably could have bought a few dozen of them.

Except that cruising for a week or two on even the largest yacht would have left them with a few too many silences to fill.

Across the way, a family had commandeered two tables and still spilled over the edges in a three-generational confusion of bodies and laughter. What would it be like to be a part of that kind of happy tangle of relations? she wondered enviously. Someone to joust with, someone to travel with. Someone else to try to talk some sense into Carter. Instead, she had a handful of disgruntled stepbrothers and sisters, all of whom wanted no part of the man they now loathed, except for maybe his money.

Larkin shook her head. No point wasting time on pointless thinking. "Our first port of call is Juneau," she said. "You can always catch up with the ship there."

"Forget Juneau. The cab driver tells me we're twenty minutes away. I'll be there."

"In that case, you'll find me on the lido deck."

"Good. Order a bottle of Clicquot. We'll drink to the future."

To the future, Carter's favorite toast. Not surprising for a man who'd made the bulk of his fortune from futures trading.

Larkin ended the call and walked through the doors that led outside onto the fantail, not sure whether she was amused or annoyed. Then again, Carter had that effect on people. He could be, by turns, infuriating, surprising, generous, charming, brilliant and astonishingly pigheaded. As a husband, he'd been a miserable failure in marriages two, three, four and, she assumed, five. As a father, he'd been like a football team—good seasons and bad seasons.

And, for the previous five years, off seasons.

She pulled her duster-style coat more tightly around her to ward off the chill and shook her head. A trip to celebrate his sixtieth birthday, he'd said, but she'd recognized it for what it was—an olive branch. A fine idea, in theory. What she and Carter were going to do with one another for a week solid, though, heaven only knew.

Staring at the islands across the bay, Larkin watched a floatplane as it dropped down from the sky and scudded along the waves. How did it feel to land on water the first time, on shifting waves instead of the solid concrete of a runway?

Like finding out she was going to be living with a new stepmother. And another. And another.

"Stop right now!"

The man's shout had Larkin whirling to see a small girl pelting out of the doors, glancing back over her shoulder and laughing. And then it seemed to happen in slow motion, the girl tripping, falling, pitching toward the deck with a yelp.

"Hey!" Reflexively, Larkin reached out to catch the wiry little body before it hit. She didn't reckon on the momentum, though, and instead wound up tumbling to the deck with her, her BlackBerry spinning away.

"Whoops." The girl grinned at her from under a mop of curly dark hair.

There was a rush of steps. "What the hell?" A man skidded to a stop and stared down at them a little out of breath. "Sophia, you know you're not supposed to run."

"*Maman* says *hell* is a bad word."

"Then I guess you shouldn't say it." He hoisted her to her feet.

His cropped hair was as dark as his daughter's, Larkin saw. Matching stubble darkened his jaw, a frankly delectable jaw with a chin that had just a hint of a cleft, the kind that made Larkin want to nibble it.

Lucky *Maman.*

He held out a hand as Larkin sat up. "Need a lift?"

He might have had the cheekbones of a model but he had the beat-up hands of a man who worked for a living, scarred, sinewy. She was prepared for his palm to feel hard and callused. She wasn't prepared for the jolt of heat that surged through her, as though he were connected to some hidden power source. She swayed as she stood.

"Easy, there. Take a minute to get your sea legs."

"We're not at sea yet."

"Which is why you should start now."

He retrieved her BlackBerry and handed it to her. An irresistible humor hovered around the corners of hi mouth, glimmered in his brown eyes. "Christopher Trask, he said. "And this little heathen, who will be apologizin any minute, is my niece, Sophia."

Niece.

"I already apologized," Sophia complained, squirming

He gave her a stern look. "What did I hear your mothe tell you about running?"

"That you were supposed to stop me," she returned with an impudent look. "Anyway, you said a bad word."

They stared at each other a moment, at an impasse. "How old are you again?" Christopher asked finally.

"You know I'm six."

"Do you want to live to blackmail again at seven? Apologize."

Sophia eyed him. "You won't tell *Maman* I was running?"

"Not if you say you're sorry." And not if she didn't out him, Larkin realized with silent laughter. "Now please apologize properly to Ms...."

"Hayes," she replied obediently. "Larkin Hayes."

Christopher folded his arms and cleared his throat.

Sophia shuffled her feet. "I'm sorry I knocked you down. I shouldn'ta been running." She looked up at Christopher beguilingly. "Can I go tell Keegan about the stuffed penguins now?"

"Sure, but don't...run," he finished as Sophia dashed back inside. He watched her for a moment, then nodded to himself as she apparently reached her destination. He turned back to Larkin, dusting off his hands. "You can see how she respects me."

Larkin gave him an amused look. "Your mastery of the situation is obvious."

"I was afraid of that." He scrubbed at his hair ruefully. "It's harder than it looks, you know. Especially when they run in packs."

"Family vacation?"

He nodded. "It sounded like a good idea at the time."

"It always does." She walked over to the rail. "I take it you don't have experience with kids?"

"Nope. Bachelor uncle. Or, I don't know, first cousin twice removed? They're my cousins' kids, whatever that makes me."

"Uncle Soft Touch?" she suggested.

"Not if I can help it." He came to a stop beside her.

"Of course not. I don't know what I was thinking," she said sweetly as she leaned on the varnished wood.

"The trick is to break their spirits while they're young."

The corner of her mouth twitched. "And I can see how good you are at it. Shouldn't you be getting back inside? Their parents must be desperate without you."

His glance at the doors was a little hunted. "I'm sure they won't miss me. I'll just soak up a little more sun."

"You're aware it's fifty-eight degrees and cloudy, right?"

"I'm an eternal optimist."

This time she grinned outright. "So how many of them are you up against?"

"Five. All under the age of seven. If you see me in a bar later mainlining Shirley Temples, you'll know I cracked."

"I'll be sure to send over some peanuts."

Gulls circled over the whitecap-dotted water. Christopher wore only khakis and a deep blue flannel shirt against the fresh breeze that sent the pennants over their heads snapping, but he seemed not to mind it.

"Do you work outside?"

He blinked. "Why do you ask?"

"You don't seem to mind the cold."

His teeth gleamed. "I run a farm in Vermont. This is balmy."

"Vermont," she said. "Maple syrup."

"You'll warm my cousin Jacob's heart. He and my aunt have a sugar bush. They make maple syrup," Christopher elaborated at her uncomprehending look.

"Seriously?"

"Well, someone's got to. Or are you one of those people who thinks that food comes from the grocery store?"

"Of course not. Everybody knows it comes from restaurant kitchens."

It was his turn to grin. "You take some keeping up with, Larkin Hayes."

"Get your running shoes handy. So what do you farm?"

"These days mostly bills."

"Not much money in that," she observed.

"There is for my creditors. For me, it's a miracle cure for being rich. Anyway, what about you? What's your story?"

Improbable, at best. "Not nearly as colorful as yours. I'm traveling with my father. It's his birthday."

"Figured it would be nice to celebrate?"

"Yes." And even nicer if Carter actually made it onto the ship.

"So where is he?"

"Oh, around," she said vaguely.

"Had to take a breather already? We haven't even sailed."

Larkin gave him a sharp look. "He's not here yet. He got delayed. We were coming from different cities." Different continents, actually, but the less said about that the better. She pushed away from the rail to walk.

Christopher ambled alongside her. "So what was your city?"

"L.A."

"Yeah? You an actress?"

She laughed. "Why would you ask that?"

Humor glimmered in his eyes. "Because you're not big enough to be on *American Gladiators*."

"It's not the size, it's the viciousness. I've got tricks up my sleeve that would turn your hair white."

"In that case, could you show me a few so I can defend myself against my nieces and nephews?"

She gave him a sly look. "I only use my powers for good."

"Oh, come on, I need all the help I can get."

"Sorry, Gladiators' code."

He shook his head sadly. "You didn't look like a cruel woman when I picked you off the deck."

"Looks can be deceiving."

"In other words, you really are an actor."

"Isn't everybody?" She glanced beyond him to see Sophia giggling at the door, next to a little boy with the same midnight hair. "I think you're being summoned."

Christopher turned to see them both waving madly at him. "Time to go play uncle," he said.

"Well, it was nice to meet you." She put out her hand. "I guess this is goodbye."

His look held pure devilry. "Just how big do you think this ocean liner is?"

Small, he thought as he followed Sophia back inside to the staterooms. With luck, as small as a tugboat. Larkin Hayes was far and away the most interesting person he'd met on the cruise so far. Oh, hell, who was he kidding? She was far and away the most interesting woman he'd met in years. Four years, to be exact. There was something about her that made it hard to look away, some inner sparkle, a confidence in the way she stood, long and slim. Not to mention the fact that she was flat-out gorgeous with that wide, generous mouth and that mane of blond hair that made a man want to sink his hands into it. It wasn't that that got to him, though (really), but the smarts. Was there anything sexier than a clever-tongued woman?

She put that intelligence to good use, he figured, judging by her outfit: pea-size diamonds in her ears, a cashmere coat and, unless he was very much mistaken, a forty-thousand-dollar Patek Philippe watch. You noticed that kind of thing when you'd spent over eleven years as a financial industry lobbyist. Between Washington and Wall

Street, he'd seen pretty much all the trappings of wealth that were out there.

Which had eventually sent him running back to the farming life he'd grown up with, but that was a different story.

And Larkin Hayes had a story. It showed in her eyes, sea green and dancing with fun, yet guarded in some indefinable way. They might have talked but she'd told him very little.

Which only made him want to find out more.

It was an ocean liner and there were only so many places to go. Sooner or later—sooner if he had anything to say about it—they'd run into each other again. Yep, by the end of the week, he was going to know Larkin Hayes a whole lot better.

"We're *moving!*"

"No standing on the deck chairs, Adam," Molly Trask reminded her grandson as they stood on their suite's veranda. Her bobbed hair, once a glossy black, had turned full silver, a color that made her eyes look even bluer. She'd stayed trim, though—anyone with a family and a business like she had spent way too much time running around to let the pounds pile on.

"I wanna see," Adam said obstinately.

"You just had your turn," Jacob Trask said, turning from where he held Adam's twin sister, Sophia, and their brother Gerard. Tall and burly as a lumberjack, Jacob looked like he could easily hold them up forever. And as their father, he probably would. "When your mama comes back from making her spa appointments, we'll go up top where we can see everything."

"But—"

He came by it honestly, Molly thought. Adam senior,

her husband, had always been impatient himself. Impatient to work, impatient to live, impatient to love. And, it seemed, impatient to die. Ten years had passed since he'd left her, suddenly and unexpectedly. Ten years and it still felt fresh. In the time since his death, she'd focused on her family, watching her sons marry and start families of their own. How her barrel-chested, booming-voiced Adam would have loved being surrounded by his half-dozen grandchildren, rolling on the floor and playing with them. Spoiling them unmercifully, no doubt.

Well, she was no slouch in the spoiling department herself. Nor, she thought, were her sons, spiriting her off on an Alaskan luxury cruise just because she'd read an article in the Sunday travel section. To see the glaciers, they said, but she knew what it was really about. It was the tenth anniversary of Adam's death, and they wanted to take her somewhere she'd be surrounded by family and things to see and do. Sweet of them, she thought fondly. They never asked, but she knew they worried and wondered why she'd never remarried. How could she explain that a love like she'd had with Adam left little room for another?

So she stood outside her plush stateroom and counted herself the luckiest woman around because she had the most precious of things—family.

She rose. "Come on, Adam, I'll take you to the top deck."

The movement took Larkin by surprise. One minute, she was sipping at her appletini and idly chatting to the couple next to her at the bar. The next, she'd realized that the pier was farther off. A lot farther off.

So that was it, then. They were under way, and Carter hadn't arrived.

It shouldn't have surprised her. It shouldn't even have made her pause. She'd known when he'd called that there was no way he was going to make it. It wasn't exactly the first time he'd promised something he hadn't come through with.

So why did she feel let down?

The reality was that she missed him. She hadn't wanted the five-year schism between them, she just hadn't been able to stand by and see him rush down the aisle half-cocked yet again. Perhaps the first time she'd watched him had been the hardest, when she'd been thirteen, pale, still grieving the loss of her mother the year before. After that, she'd gotten better at it, and it had gotten easier. She'd grown accustomed to the cycle, learned how to get used to the new faces in the house but not attached.

In marriage, Carter had taught her hope, but he'd also taught her cynicism. With her mother, it had been ideal. In the marriages since, the affection, the white lace and taffeta had a way of morphing all too soon to arguments and hostility, to an angry crescendo followed by a few months of quiet after the wife of the moment had swept out and before the next began to make his eyes twinkle. Over and over Larkin had watched it happen—the rash decisions, the headlong rush, the racing disillusionment, like high-speed footage of the phases of the moon. Marry in haste, repent in court. The last time, though, at twenty-two, she'd refused to sit by and watch it all play out again.

And she'd told him why.

Carter hadn't taken it well. The words had been bitter and echoed through the silence between them in the years since.

The partially successful legal battle to break his prenuptial agreement had lasted longer than the marriage, or so she'd heard. There'd been no rumors of a new Mrs. Hayes on the horizon. Perhaps, approaching sixty, widowed and with four subsequent divorces under his belt, Carter had finally decided to take a breather. His voice on the phone that hot August morning a few weeks before had almost made her drop the handset in shock, but she'd listened. Come with me, he'd said. We'll have fun.

A chance to get through to him, Larkin had thought, a chance to make things right. Of course, making things right was kind of hard to do with someone who wasn't there.

She downed the rest of her drink and rose.

"I thought you were going to order champagne," a voice said behind her.

And in a rush of gladness, Larkin turned to see her father face-to-face for the first time in five years.

He looked the same, she realized in surprise. Oh, a pound or two more, maybe, and a bit less hair, but there was still a spark of enthusiasm in his eyes, an energy in the way he moved. Carter Hayes had grown older, perhaps, but on the dawn of his sixtieth birthday, he was not yet old.

He pulled her to him for a hug.

"I thought you'd missed the boat," she said into his shoulder.

"I told you I'd make it. One of these days you should learn to trust me." He held on a moment more, then released her. "So," he said as he pulled out a chair, "where's that bubbly?"

"Look at this place," Christopher said as he walked through the open door of his cousin Gabe's suite. "You could fit my room in here three times and still have some space left over."

"Is it our fault we know how to live in style?" Gabe stepped in from the veranda.

"It's not the knowing that's the problem," Christopher told him.

The color scheme was tones of peach and gold, to contrast with the ocean blues. Mirrors on one wall made the spacious suite look even bigger. Below the mirrored panels, the bed held pride of place with its snowy linens, puffy duvet and embarrassment of pillows. The built-in couch that ran along the opposite wall before curving out around the broad glass coffee table would hold three or four visitors, or sleep his cousin's two rambunctious boys, unless they wanted to curl up in the armchairs that finished off the conversational grouping. But it was the wall of windows giving out onto the broad veranda that truly spoke of luxury. It was the windows that brought the sea inside.

"So your room's small?" Gabe asked.

"Not so much. It's at least the size of your bathroom."

"That's what you get for taking over the room of a half-broke public servant." Gabe was referring to his firefighter brother, Nick, who'd had to cancel his trip because of his wife's unexpected pregnancy.

"You're right. I should have held out on coming until you agreed to swap me for your room."

"You'd have held out a long time."

"How's Sloane doing, anyway?" Christopher asked.

"Still the size of a house, last time I heard." Gabe's eyes twinkled. "Twins will do that to you."

They stepped outside into the fresh sea air.

"Hi, Christopher." Gabe's wife, Hadley, stood at the rail with their sons, Keegan and Kelsey, her pale hair blowing in the breeze. The slender blonde gave an impression of fragility, but there was a core of strength there as well. And excitement to rival that of her sons, he saw as she waved at the pine-covered islands that dotted the waterway. "Have you ever seen anything so gorgeous?" she demanded.

Gabe stepped forward and kissed her. "Yes."

She made a show of rolling her eyes, but she didn't move away, Christopher noticed. "I'm going to take the boys down to play with the other kids and leave you two to relax. There's some sort of rumor about stuffed penguins somewhere on the ship."

Gabe dropped a kiss on her temple. "I have a better idea. Let Uncle Christopher show them the penguins, and you can help me find my phone."

"You've lost your phone?" She frowned. "When? Do you remember where you saw it last?"

"On the bed, I think. Under the pillows. Maybe under the covers."

"I'll find it, Dad." Keegan raced inside and began throwing pillows industriously off the bed, chiefly in the direction of his little brother Kelsey, Christopher noticed. Who threw them right back.

"Now you've done it," Hadley said, as the pillow fight escalated.

Gabe put his hands up. "You can't blame me for trying."

"Thanks for the thought." She leaned in and kissed him thoroughly just before the chorus of yelps started inside. "I'd better get in there before they tear the place up. You two have fun."

Gabe walked in and supervised pillow cleanup, then watched her herd the boys out the door. He headed back outside, this time with the addition of a couple of beers.

"Quite a woman you've got there," Christopher said, taking one.

"Ain't she, though?" Gabe Trask sat back in one of the deck chairs with a beatific smile.

"Too bad kids put a hitch in the cruise romance stuff."

"Not at all." Gabe twisted the cap off his beer and took a swallow. "You just get friendly Uncle Christopher to take them for a walk. A really long walk."

Christopher eyed him. "What's it worth to you?"

"You're not going to make me call in a marker, are you? Who was it who got you the date with Lulu Simmons?"

"Did you forget how that turned out?"

"It's not my fault that you shut the door on her skirt and ripped her—"

Christopher winced. "Can we talk about something besides my worst high-school moments?"

Gabe gave him a sunny grin. "But it gives us so much to talk about."

"How about your life as a hotel magnate and sexually deprived father of two?"

"Funny thing about hotels," Gabe said thoughtfully, "all those beds. I'm betting you're more sexually deprived than I am."

"It's a depressing thought, but you're probably right."

"You ever hear from Nicole at all?"

"Not since the divorce came through. I see her in a magazine every now and again."

"It's been, what, four years? How long since you've had a date?"

"It's been, what, four years?" Christopher gave a faint smile. "The goats are beginning to look really good."

"Sick bastard," Gabe said. "How is life on the farm, anyway?"

Christopher took a swallow of beer. "Hey, how about those Red Sox?"

"I take it that means not so good?"

"There's a reason they call it subsistence farming. Although I'm not doing all that well on the subsisting side."

"That's because you blow all your money on hay parties."

Once, money hadn't been a problem, back when he'd been working in D.C., living in the corridors of power with a glossy model wife, an architecturally notable condo on the water, a Manhattan apartment and a stock portfolio that was the envy of any broker. What did it mean that he'd spent a dozen years in pursuit of a goal, only to realize it was the wrong goal, a dozen years in pursuit of the perfect life, only to realize that it was the wrong life?

It had taken him only a few weeks to be sure that farming was what he wanted. He couldn't say how long it had taken Nicole to know it wasn't. The drift had been gradual. A modeling job here and there. Weekends in Washington and New York with her friends, then full weeks. Then more.

It had taken a while for him to clue in enough to call it quits. Of course, by that time it had become pretty clear that without the endless round of parties and receptions and dinners, there was little between them. As with a juggler, it had been the furious motion that had given the illusion of substance. Once the motion had stopped, there were only a few small balls on the ground. Or knives, more like, he thought, remembering the acrimonious end.

"So how serious is it?"

Christopher looked out at a hawk circling over a stand of pines on a passing island. "Pretty damned. When I get back, I brush up my resume and start getting the place ready to go up on the block."

"What the… But what about that deal with Pure Foods you were working on?"

"I'm still working on it. A year and a half into it and we're no closer to inking a supply agreement than we were at the start." He rose and walked to the rail. "Their northeast division has twelve grocery stores across New England. I doubled the size of my herd to be able to supply them with the amount of product they wanted. I've got *chèvre* coming out of my ears, but now they're dragging their feet and telling me I need to be certified by some sustainable agriculture group before they'll start buying from me. That's going to cost a few grand and take at least another six months. In the meantime, the money just keeps bleeding away."

"Get a loan to tide you over."

"Gabe, don't you get it?" he said sharply. "I can't. I'm cut off at the bank. The money's gone, all of it. Even if Pure Foods comes through, it still might be too little, too late."

"Borrow money from the family."

"From who? My mom and dad are retired. Molly and Jacob are just barely running in the black after they lost all those trees. You and Hadley are still paying off the note on that national historic landmark you run." He shook his head. "I'm out of options, Gabe. Face it. I have."

"What about—"

"Give it a rest," he snapped. Letting out a long, slow breath, he counted to three. "Look, I just want to have a week here to relax and not think about it, okay? Not worry about how to pay the feed bill, not wonder if my payroll checks are going to bounce. Just forget it all and…chill."

Gabe stared at him for a long moment and then nodded slowly. "You got it, Vanilla Ice. Just one more thing."

"What?"

"I think it's going to take a few more beers to do it right."

Christopher relaxed and dredged up a smile from somewhere. "You know, you're probably right." He came back to his chair and picked up his beer to take a drink, then stopped. "Vanilla Ice?"

Gabe smiled broadly. "I'm thinking somewhere inside you there's a blonde."

Chapter Two

"So how did you manage to get them to let you on?" Larkin asked Carter as a white-jacketed waiter appeared from behind them to top off their wineglasses. The main dining room filled the stern of the ship. Chandeliers hung from the high ceiling, crystal gleamed by candlelight. A wall of windows ran around the edge of the room, revealing the rocks and pines of the Alaskan coast in the preternatural 9:00 p.m. daylight.

"How did I get on? I had to run for it. Paid a couple of stevedores a day's wages to carry my bags. A bargain, if you ask me."

"And they let you through security and customs?"

He raised his glass. "Amazing how a few tips will grease the skids. I paid, we all ran and I got there just as they were starting to pull the gangway in."

It was impossible to miss the gleam in his eyes. "You enjoyed it."

"Anyone can do things the easy way," he said by way of answer as their waiter set appetizers of saffron langoustine in puff pastry before them.

Larkin's lips curved. "So where were you coming from this time?"

"Shenzhen, China. There's a factory out there I wanted to get a look at."

"A factory? I thought you worked the market."

He forked up a langoustine. "I've been dipping into a little bit of venture cap activity the past few years. I'm looking at funding a company with operations out there."

"You're dealing with actual companies now? I thought you said hands-on stuff was for suckers," she said, cutting into her puff pastry.

Carter shrugged. "Everything gets boring after a while, even making money."

Fork in hand, Larkin stared. "Wait a minute, you can't be my father. You must be an impostor."

"Don't get me wrong, I still like working the market. That's never going to go away. But I need a change of pace. Something different."

"And was the factory different?"

"That's one word for it," he said in amusement.

"I take it you're going to hold on to your money for now."

"You take it right." He took a swallow of wine. "Speaking of money, I talked with Walter a couple of weeks ago."

At the name of her father's lawyer—and her trust-fund administrator—Larkin glanced up. "Is that how you knew where to find me?"

Carter nodded. "He tells me your fund is getting pretty low. Says you've been tapping into the principal."

She flushed. "Not much. I'm doing all right." Okay, maybe that was overstating the case a little. The fund she'd come into when she'd turned eighteen hadn't been enormous, and she could have been smarter in the way she'd managed it. She'd spent the better part of her early twenties living in one city after another, until one day she'd realized that she wasn't looking for a home, she was looking for herself. That hadn't made what she was looking for any easier to find, but it made it easier to stay in one place.

"You need more money?" Carter asked.

"I seem to remember you telling me once I needed to get a job," she said. "I got one."

"I heard. Modeling, right? I had the impression you were dabbling more than anything."

"I'm happy to dabble for a thousand dollars an hour." She gave a faint smile. "There's a certain cachet to being the daughter of somebody who shows up on the power lists from time to time."

"Nice to know I can be helpful," Carter said dryly.

For a few moments they just toyed with the food on their plates. Larkin was the first to jump.

"So what made you pick up the phone?"

"Outside of the fact that we haven't spoken in over five years?"

She looked down at the tablecloth. "I never wanted that to happen."

"Neither did I." Long seconds went by. "I suppose you heard that Celine and I split up."

Larkin didn't say anything.

"It's killing you, isn't it?" Carter said.

"What?"

"Not saying 'I told you so.'"

She looked at him directly. "That was never what it was about."

"What was it about?"

"Not wanting to see you make another mistake. Wanting you to be fair to yourself for once, to look at a wife as closely as you did a stock." She stopped, aware she'd gone too far—and far too soon. "I'm sorry. This isn't the place or the time…"

He watched her, eyes steady. "You've grown up."

"Five years will do that."

"I'm sorry I missed it."

"You could have called sooner."

"So could you."

"Celine," she said simply.

He sighed and looked out the window at the shoreline, white sand broken up with the dark lines of beached logs.

Bitter words, bitter times, hard to get past. Larkin remembered staring at the invitation written on handcrafted linen paper, announcing Carter's impending wedding to a woman she'd distrusted on sight. Don't do this, she'd pleaded. Give it time, for once. The argument had escalated, somehow turning back on her. Suddenly it wasn't about Celine being after his money; it was about Larkin. For every point she'd taken Carter to task on, he'd returned a barb that had unerringly struck home. She had no business accusing him of being rash and impulsive when she'd never once finished anything. Who was she to talk about Celine when she'd never done anything constructive herself?

The battle had reverberated through both of their lives long after the echoes of the words had faded away. She hadn't expected it to last, but somehow the years had worn on. And now, it appeared, bridging the gap wasn't going to be as easy as either of them had hoped.

The silence stretched out as the waiters removed their plates and set out their entrées, chateaubriand for Carter and butter-poached lobster for Larkin. In the background, the pianist played "Blue Moon." Across the room there was a burst of laughter from a large table, the enormous family she'd seen that afternoon. That was how it should be, she thought. Not silence but joy.

They were all grouped together any old way, brothers and sisters, fathers and daughters. The silver-haired matriarch threw back her head in delighted laughter. Larkin glanced over and realized that Carter was watching them, as well, her own wistfulness mirrored in his eyes. Once upon a time they'd been a family like that.

Once upon a time, when her mother had been alive.

Abruptly she had to get out. "Excuse me." She rose. "I'll be right back."

In the ladies' room, she washed her hands in cold water, touching her cool fingertips to her forehead, adjusting the straps of her ruby silk halter dress. Fifteen years had passed since Beth Hayes had been killed by a drunk driver. Months at a time could pass without Larkin thinking of her, but every once in a while, like an ambush, she'd find herself overwhelmed by a wave of loss, an absence screamingly present.

She shook her head. Pointless to think of what might have been. Carter had done what he'd been able to, and if it had left her permanently wary of any and all relationships, that was her problem.

She ran her fingers through her hair and walked out the door.

Her destination was the dining room. Somehow, though, she found herself climbing the stairs that led to the fantail, instead, stepping outside to gulp deep breaths of the cool air. To either side, tree-covered mountains rose straight up from the water in a landscape that looked too wild for human habitation. The sun was finally setting, its ruddy rays slanting across the deck. The space was empty, quiet, with just the breeze for company.

Something different, Carter had said. Larkin knew how he felt. The restlessness had been brewing for months. Usually when it hit, she moved to another city, but she'd sworn off that. A change of scenery wasn't the cure. She needed something more.

There was a sound behind her. "I thought that was you," a voice said.

And she turned to see Christopher Trask.

She'd breathe, Larkin thought, in a moment. When she'd met him that afternoon, he'd been casual, appealingly rumpled. Now he stood before her in black slacks and a charcoal-gray silk shirt that made his shoulders look very wide. The effect was simple, sophisticated and sexy as hell. The man she'd met that afternoon clearly worked with his hands; the man before her belonged in an expensive gallery or on the scene of a sleek nightclub so new that celebrities didn't even know about it.

He grinned. "I told you the ship wasn't that big."

She turned to face him, her back to the rail. "Nice to see you've survived so far."

"Nice to see you, period," he said. "Dinner dress suits you."

"You clean up pretty well yourself."

"I do my best. So how's the first night aboard going?"

"It's been…interesting," she decided.

"It can't be too interesting if you're standing up here all alone. Didn't your father make it onto the ship? I thought I saw you with him earlier."

"Oh, he's here," she said. "Back in the dining room, actually. I just wanted to step outside for a minute. I just can't get over all the daylight."

He stepped closer to her. "It's that whole midnight sun thing. It must make it hard on kids. No sneaking out at night."

"And why do I think that that was an integral part of your repertoire growing up?" she asked, slanting a look at him.

"Ah, come on, it's a part of summer, like watermelon and baseball. Are you telling me you never snuck out at night when everyone else was asleep? Just to see what it felt like to be outside and on your own when nobody knew about it?"

She could feel that sense of freedom beckoning just outside the window, that breathless sense of adventure. Or maybe she just felt breathless because he was so near, close enough she could feel the heat from his body.

"You've sneaked out now, haven't you?" His voice was low. "You're supposed to be in at dinner but you're here."

"I just—" *Wanted something different.* "Wanted some air. What are you doing up here?"

"I saw you." The sunset turned his skin copper and made his eyes look dark. For an instant, she couldn't look away. For a humming moment, a kind of a pure, distilled need surged between them. On a ship with three thousand other people, it felt like they were alone in the fading light. She could get lost in this man, Larkin thought suddenly.

She swallowed. "I should get back," she said and turned to the doors. The motion of the ship sent her steps off course.

Christopher caught her arm to stabilize her. "Careful."

She felt the imprint of each individual finger on her skin, warm, distinct from the growing chill in the air. Anticipation jumped in her stomach. *Careful.*

"You don't want to fall," he added softly, slipping his fingers down to her hand and raising it to his lips.

Heat bloomed within her. The seconds spun out as it flared into desire, and all she could do was stare. There was something hypnotic about his eyes, the warmth of his lips against her hand, something that made it impossible to think of anything except how they would feel against hers. She didn't intend to lean in toward him. She simply had no choice.

His mouth was soft on hers. It was barely a kiss, just a light brush, yet she felt it everywhere. That so little could take her so far would have been terrifying if she'd been able to think of anything except the flush of heat, the shiver of excitement, the coursing of a need that could become all-consuming.

He hadn't moved to hold her. He didn't touch her otherwise except for that tantalizing brush of lips, that light graze that fired up every neuron in her body, making her pulse with the need for more. It was tease. It was invitation.

It was promise.

The restlessness she'd been feeling flared into hunger. Intellectually, she knew that whatever it was she yearned for couldn't come from another person, any more than a quartet of wives had done it for her father. But she wanted Christopher Trask, oh, she wanted him.

Behind them, the doors opened and a chattering group of people walked out. "Whoops," someone said loudly, "looks like we're interrupting."

It had her stepping back, her eyes flying open only to leave her feeling that she was still in a dream. "Well," she said blankly.

"I was thinking more along the lines of 'wow.'"

Larkin shook her head to get her mind working again. "I should…"

"Have a drink with me," he supplied.

Forget about the drink, she just wanted him. But she had obligations. "It's the first night. I haven't seen my father in forever. I need to go back in."

Christopher nodded and touched his hand lightly to the small of her back as they started toward the doors. "Later, then."

Just a flick of a glance from him was all it took to start the pull again, but she couldn't just disappear on Carter. She wasn't twenty years old and here to find a guy to hook up with.

But what a guy.

She moved a little bit away from him as they walked through the doors to the dining room, but when she glanced toward her table, she stopped.

"What?"

"My father's gone."

"You sure you've got the right table? It's a big dining room."

"Of course it's the right table. Over by the window, beyond the planter."

Christopher looked where she gestured and raised his eyebrows. "You were gone a long time. Maybe he had to go see a man about a dog."

"I suppose," she said, and hesitated. "Let me see how dinner goes. Maybe we can have that drink after all."

"Better yet, come to our table."

"But my fath—"

"At least until he comes back. You can protect me from the nieces and nephews. Show off some of your *American Gladiators* chops." He steered them that way before she could protest further.

She shouldn't have been even remotely surprised that he walked up to the family at the big table. Up close, the sense of fun and pleasure shimmered around them. Although they were finishing up dessert and coffee, nearly everyone in the Trask family appeared to be more interested in talking and laughing than in food. A blond beach-boy type held a woman on his lap—girlfriend or wife, judging by the kiss he planted on her hair. A pair of men with enough similarity in their dark good looks to make them brothers held an energetic debate about baseball and someone named Papi. Sophia was absorbed in a fast, complicated version of patty-cake with a tow-headed little boy who was the spitting image of the delicate-looking white blonde next to her, who in turn laughed with a mischievous-looking woman with a pixie's cap of brunette curls. It was a chaotic, all-ages blend of people thoroughly enjoying being together.

"Hi, Larkin!" Sophia broke off her hand-slapping to wave.

"Hey, guys," Christopher said to them all. "I brought a stowaway for dessert. This is Larkin. Let's see, Larkin, this is my sister Lainie and her husband J.J.—" He pointed to the beach boy. "You know Sophia, and she's playing with Kelsey, who's the son of Hadley, there, and my cousin Gabe." One of the dark-haired men raised his hand. "The guy next to him is my other cousin Jacob, and his wife Celie's the one talking to Hadley, and—"

"Stop, Christopher," protested Celie, the brunette pixie. "You've got her head spinning. Just let the poor thing sit." A hint of a French accent colored her words.

"So where's Aunt Molly?" Christopher asked, standing near Larkin.

"She went to the ladies' room. A while ago, now that I think about it. She should be back soon."

"In fact, she's here now," said an amused voice.

Larkin turned, and found herself startled into silence. There was no doubt where the Trask boys had gotten their good looks. Molly Trask's face held a quiet loveliness, enough to have attracted an escort, Larkin saw. She extended her hand. "I'm Larkin."

"The one who caught Sophia? I'm so pleased to meet you, Larkin," Molly said warmly. "I'm Molly Trask. And this is—"

"My father—"

"Carter Hayes," Christopher said simultaneously.

"What?" Larkin whipped her head around to stare at him.

"What are you doing over here?" Carter asked.

"You weren't at the table. I came over with—" She shook her head. "Never mind."

"This is Larkin, my daughter," Carter told Molly.

"We're going to need a bigger table," Gabe said.

There was an after-dinner quiet to the decks as they all walked back to their rooms. The group of them had lingered over coffee and liqueur until the children had started yawning, worn out by the excitement of the day. Now Jacob carried his youngest son while Celie and Hadley shepherded the rest.

"We'll be leaving at nine tomorrow morning for the glacier flight," Carter said to everyone as they stepped out of the elevator. "We've got four open seats, so whoever wants to come is welcome."

Christopher wasn't surprised that Carter and Larkin had rooms on the luxury deck. Carter probably could have booked every suite on the ship with his pocket change alone. He walked along with Molly now, to escort her to her room on the portside hallway. Judging by the weather eye Jacob gave him as the rest of the family followed, that was all he was going to do.

"I guess we're on our own," Christopher said to Larkin as they stood at the entrance to the starboard hallway. "I take it you guys are down here?"

"I am. Carter's on the other hall. We only got our reservations a few weeks ago. We had to take what they had."

He nodded. "It's still early. How about that drink?"

"I don't think so."

There was a kind of tension gathered about her. It was different than the restless curiosity he'd sensed on the fantail. It hadn't come from the kiss, that much he was sure of. He knew when he held a willing woman in his arms. Somewhere around the time Carter had shown up, though, it had started to simmer. Christopher found himself subtly on edge. Something was going on with her, and he wasn't the type of man to just let it go.

"It's a big ship. We don't have to go to a bar. There are other things to do, the casino, the piano lounge, the show. What do you think?"

"You want to know what I think?" Larkin asked coolly. "I think it's very strange that a farmer from Vermont would recognize a man like Carter Hayes." She turned down the hallway toward her room.

Christopher blinked and followed. "It shouldn't be all that surprising. He's a prominent guy."

"Only in some circles." They moved aside for an older couple to pass. "Carter lives pretty quietly. He doesn't show up in the news. It's not like he's Malcolm Forbes or Warren Buffett."

"I think you underestimate him."

"Apparently, I underestimate farmers in Vermont," Larkin returned. "Here I figured you spent your time talking about the price of grain, not futures traders. Who knew?"

"We do talk about the price of grain. And at my old job, we talked about futures traders like Carter."

"Your old job?" She stopped to stare at him.

"I was a lobbyist for the financial industry."

"A lobbi—" Suspicion bloomed into anger. And betrayal. "So you know who Carter is." Probably right down to his net worth, Larkin thought as she strode down to her door, key card in hand.

"I followed the industry, and Carter was a part of it," Christopher responded. "I don't get what the problem is here."

"Let me catch up a minute. You were a Washington mover and shaker, and then one day you just decided to throw it all away to become a farmer?"

"I wouldn't use the words *throwing it all away*," he said curtly. "I decided I wanted something else."

"Except it sounds like that something else isn't treating you too well."

A muscle jumped in his jaw. "If you knew anything about farming, you'd know that's pretty common."

"How convenient for you that you met me."

He frowned. "Meaning?"

Larkin gave him a bright, hard, merciless smile. "It's funny how it works when you're the daughter of a man like Carter. The whole world wants to be your best friend. Every guy with any ambition wants to date you—hell, forget dating, they want marriage, as long as it comes with a piece of the pie. They want to get close to the man. I've been offered five-carat diamond engagement rings." She ran her key card and opened her door. "And you thought you were making progress with just a kiss or two?"

She started to walk inside but he caught at her shoulder. "That's nuts. Paranoid."

She whirled on him. "You want a list of the times it happened?" She'd had a lifetime of sharp-eyed people who wanted to use her to get close to Carter and his money.

She just hadn't expected Christopher to be one of them.

"Are you saying I kissed you because of Carter?" Christopher asked tightly, anger stirring in his words.

"Are you trying to say it had nothing to do with it?" She'd felt the chemistry when they'd met, but between the flirtation of the afternoon and the raging need that had flared that evening lay a vast gulf. Between the flirtation of the afternoon and the heat of the night, Christopher had seen her with Carter. Christopher, who knew exactly who Carter Hayes was, and how much money he had. "Why didn't you tell me you recognized Carter?" she demanded, striding inside.

He stalked after her. "Because I didn't. When I saw you guys before, you were down the hall. I didn't get a good look."

"Yeah, right."

There was a subtle change in his stance, even though he didn't move. If she'd been paying attention, Larkin would have seen it. "So I'm a hustler now, is that it?" he demanded.

Too caught up in her own fury, she didn't register the gathering storm. "You tell me. All I know is that it's kind of funny how things changed. One minute, you're just some guy chatting on deck. Then you see me with Carter— or excuse me, *someone,*" she qualified elaborately, missing the narrowing of his eyes, "and suddenly the next time we're together you go all continental with the hand kissing and the heavy stares and..." She swallowed, remembering the flare of heat and need, noticing for the first time the palpable tension that hung around him.

"And?" he bit off, a dangerous flash in his eyes.

She flushed. "And nothing. If you want to try to get to Carter through me, you're going to have to do a lot more than just kiss my hand."

"Gladly." And before she knew what he was about, he'd dragged her to him, lips coming down hot and possessive on hers.

This wasn't a soft whisper of invitation; it wasn't about tempting. This was frustration and challenge, anger and need. It was an all-out assault on her senses. Desire whipped through her in those first few stunned seconds, and she was helpless to do anything but feel. Every fiber of her being focused on the hot press of his mouth, the demand of his hands, the male flavor of him as her lips parted and he took them both deeper.

He kissed her with an almost arrogant ownership, as though he'd already plundered every inch of her body. As though he already knew exactly how she liked to be touched.

And he did.

The ship moved beneath them, but it was the arousal surging through her veins that had her clinging to him as she swayed against him on legs that would no longer hold her. The feel of his palms running over her bare shoulders made her shiver. She breathed in, open mouth to his, as though it was him she needed, more than sustenance, more than air. Her world had reduced to just this: his lips, his hands, his body against her.

He had no business kissing her like this, Christopher knew. But he'd been holding back practically since he'd first seen her. Somewhere along the line, the goading had loosened the tight grip he kept on his control. It wasn't just irritation at the insult that had the passion and frustration inside him bubbling over. He needed more. He needed for her to acknowledge this pull between them. He needed to know that it clawed at her, too.

She was soft and pliant against him. The silken strands of her hair brushed at his cheek. She tasted dark and sweet and sinfully delicious, like some stolen treat to be scooped up with a fingertip and savored.

He worked his way across her cheek to the line of her jaw, tasting her skin. With a helpless noise, she let her head fall back. He pressed his lips against the curving line of her throat, inhaling her scent, half devouring her. The desire drummed through him, the need to take, the compulsion to satisfy the howling demand.

She wrapped herself around him, mouth moving avidly under his, making soft purring noises of pleasure.

He could take her at this moment, he knew. The bed was mere steps away. He could have them both naked in seconds and be sliding into that purely female softness, sliding into heat and sensation and inevitability to take them both over the edge. Instead, he made himself pull away, leaving her to stare at him, eyes dazed, mouth swollen from his.

"Wha…" She blinked. "I…"

"Trust me, Larkin." He looked down at her. "Whatever happens between you and me has absolutely nothing to do with Carter."

And he pulled open the door and walked away.

While he still could.

Chapter Three

Juneau was possibly the narrowest city Larkin had ever seen, clinging stubbornly to the tiny strip of flat ground that lay between the Gastineau Channel and the high mountains that rose abruptly a few hundred yards inland. What it lacked in width, it tried to make up for in length, stretching out along both sides of the inlet.

Larkin walked down the gangway, buttoning her coat against the chilly air. There must have been other days she'd started the day so cranky, but she couldn't remember when.

"Flying over glaciers," Carter said from behind her. "Now there's something you don't do every day."

"Forget about the glaciers. Let the Trasks entertain themselves. We should do the zip line," Larkin said.

"What's a zip line?"

Strenuous, risky, adrenaline-laced. Just the ticket for the mood she was in. "It'll be fun. You'll see."

"Next time. For now, we've got a plane and pilot to ourselves for the day. We'll see parts of Alaska you can't get to on foot."

Impatient to the last, Carter had hired a private plane and pilot. Forget about group excursions, he'd said. They'd see what they wanted to see, when they wanted to see it.

Them, and now their new guests.

Molly Trask stood on the pier beyond the bottom of the gangway, her cheeks pretty and pink with cold. "Good morning," she called out as they approached.

Great, Larkin thought. Carter's new crush.

"Ready to walk on a glacier?" Carter asked.

Molly shook her head. "I must be out of my mind. I couldn't walk without help across a solid deck last night. God only knows how I'm going to do it on a sheet of ice."

"I guess I'll just have to keep an eye on you."

"You don't have to do that."

"Trust me, it won't be a hardship," Carter assured her. "Keeping an eye on you will be the easiest day's work I've ever done."

Molly blinked. "Oh. Well." The pink that crept over her cheeks had nothing to do with cold. Flustered, she turned to the steep peaks that rose behind city.

"How do you like Alaska?" Carter asked, amused.

"Gorgeous," she said. "It's even more beautiful than home, and I never thought I'd say that."

"Where's home?"

"Vermont."

"Well, how about that? I'm from your neck of the woods."

"Really? Where?" She pulled out a pair of sunglasses.

He rubbed his chin. "Manhattan."

"I'm not sure that qualifies as my neck of the woods," she said, sliding the glasses on.

"Are you kidding? It's the Northeast. We're practically neighbors."

Her lips twitched. "I see. Well, next time you need a cup of sugar, feel free to stop by."

"I'll do that. So is anybody else coming?"

"Christopher should be along in just a minute."

Christopher, Larkin thought, gritting her teeth. *Of course.*

"What about the rest?" Carter asked.

"Gabriel and Jacob and their families just left to go dogsledding. The kids have been talking about it for weeks. Lainie and J.J. decided to do the zip line."

"Just what the heck is a zip line, anyway? Larkin's pushing me to do it."

Molly patted his arm. "Better not to ask," she advised.

"Is this something I should know about?"

"Probably best that you don't."

He glanced suspiciously at Larkin, who gave him her most innocent look. "It's a sad day when you find out that you can't trust your own child."

"She didn't say you wouldn't have fun," Larkin pointed out.

Carter glanced over to the transportation apron where the excursion buses were lined up, then turned back to Larkin. "There's supposed to be a van here to take us to the airstrip. We'll go find it and check in with the driver. You wait for Christopher. We should be down at the far end, past all the buses." He held out his arm for Molly. "So tell me what you do with yourself all day up in Vermont."

Larkin watched them walk off and resisted the urge to sigh. If Carter wanted to have a shipboard romance, he would. Being an adult was about learning to release what you couldn't control, and she couldn't control Carter any more than she could the tides. If he was set on pursuing Molly Trask, Larkin had no business trying to dissuade him.

Christopher Trask, now, she definitely had business with him.

She'd spent a long, sleepless night being rocked by the motion of the ship while she imagined wreaking detailed vengeance on him. The death by paper cuts scenario had pleased her most. Unfortunately, no matter how furious she was with him, down beneath it all the wanting still thrummed. And it was for that that she cursed him most of all. He'd made her yearn, taken her to surrender, and they both knew it.

And despite it all, she still wanted him.

Where was a voodoo doll when you needed one, Larkin wondered, jamming her hands in her pockets. Even something to throw would make her feel better. Especially if it was at Christopher Trask's head.

She pulled out her BlackBerry to check messages.

It was a testament to the depth of her hostility that she knew, somehow, when he was approaching. Definitely hostility, for all that it felt like a buzz of anticipation. She turned back toward the *Alaskan Voyager.*

It was that easy stride that gave him away. He walked with the relaxed, confident self-possession of an athlete. He wore a leather bomber jacket over jeans and a thick cream colored fisherman's sweater. A navy-blue watch cap sat atop his head. When he saw her, he gave that killer smile. Larkin found herself responding reflexively before she could remind herself that she hated him.

"Hey," he said as he stopped before her. "Where's everybody else?"

"Carter and Molly went to look for the van." She stood there with her arms crossed before her, shoulders square and stiff. "They told me to wait for you. Lucky me."

His smile was very wide. "No. Lucky me."

* * *

She was seriously ticked, Christopher thought. Every movement of her body shouted it. Fair enough. He'd been pretty ticked off himself. The clash of wills had drawn blood—and heated it—on both sides. The question was, what happened next?

She stood in her long black coat and jeans, along with one of those round white fur hats that made her look like some expatriate czarina. Silver teardrops swung at her ears. The wind tossed around the honey-gold strands of her hair and brought out a flush of cold in her cheeks. And maybe the sparkle in her eyes was at the thought of telling him to go to the devil, but he'd take it as long as she kept looking like that.

Anyway, he was betting he could talk her out of being mad.

"So this is Juneau, huh?"

"Feel free to stick around and explore," she said. "We'll just head on out to the airfield."

"No way, we've got glaciers to see. Where's the bus?"

"Down near the end, Carter said." She started walking without looking to see that he followed. He saw her smother a yawn.

"How did you sleep?" he asked.

She shot him a venomous look. "Never better. And you?"

"I kind of liked it." Even if it had taken him a couple of hours to drift off. "Sort of like sleeping in a hammock, with all that swaying. And then I wake up and there's someone knocking on the door and bringing me coffee. I mean, what's not to like?"

"I'm sure if you went back to your cabin right now, someone would bring you coffee again. Why don't you go on board and find out?"

"I'd say nice try, but that wasn't even a very good one.

What are you pissed off about," he added, "that I kissed you last night or that you liked it?"

"Does the caveman routine usually work for you?" she asked pleasantly.

"It's not my usual MO, but I figured you deserved something special."

"Pardon me for not appreciating it."

"You wanted a demonstration. I figured the least I could do was oblige." And it hadn't been a hardship he thought, watching her now and remembering the scent of her skin. Walking away when she'd been heated and avid against him had been one of the hardest things he'd ever done. And she remembered it, too. He saw those green eyes darken before she shook her head and turned away.

"I don't know why I'm even bothering talking to you," she muttered.

"Because it's a gorgeous morning. We're in an incredible place. You're too smart to spend the day pouting."

"I don't pout," she returned in outrage.

"My mistake," he said. "Isn't that the van?" He pointed toward the minibus where Carter and Molly waited, already inside.

At the airstrip, they pulled up to an unprepossessing vinyl-sided building with a green sign that said Taku Glacier Excursions. As soon as the minibus doors opened, a staffer who looked like she was fourteen—if she was lucky—stepped on board. "Hi, everyone," she said as they rose. "I'm Amy."

Carter rose. "I'm Carter Hayes, the one who rented the plane. We've brought along a couple more people than we were planning, but it shouldn't be an issue. There's room."

"Actually," she shifted uncomfortably, "we've sort of got a problem."

"We?" Carter repeated. "What kind of problem do *we* have?"

"Uh, the plane's not here."

Carter's brows lowered a fraction. "I had my assistant pay for it a month ago. What do you mean it's not here?"

The girl coughed. "A couple of climbers got lost on Denali. There's a big search under way, and the, uh, plane that was supposed to take you to the glaciers is part of it. We've got a substitute, though," she rushed to add. "A local 'copter pilot, Buck Matthews, is going to take you up."

Buck Matthews, Larkin thought, looking out on the pads where the helicopters crouched like metal and Plexiglas dragonflies. Perfect. "Dad, maybe we ought to skip it."

"I think you'll really like the helicopter," Amy told her. "It's better than the plane because you can hover over anything you want to see. And Buck's been flying for years. He really knows the area. Oh—" she paused "—you don't have any problems with animals, right?" Puzzled, they shook their heads and Amy exhaled in relief. "Great, let's get you into some glacier boots, and then you can follow me out to the helicopter pad."

The boots were black and puffy and slipped over their regular shoes. Larkin sensed rather than heard Christopher sit on the bench beside her as she strapped hers on.

"It's a good look for you," he said. "Very stylish."

She scowled at him and rose to follow Amy out to the helicopter pad.

"It kind of gives you that astronaut experience, doesn't it?" Christopher asked. When she didn't answer, he leaned in. "You're going to have to break down and talk to me sometime."

"That's where you're wrong," she said, and cursed herself the minute the words were out of her mouth.

His grin flashed. "Like I said." He winked as he walked past her.

The closer they got to the helicopter, the more uneasy Larkin became. She'd been expecting a nice twin-engine Cessna with individual seats. Instead, they had a helicopter that looked like it had been borrowed from a TV traffic report team in Anchorage.

Assuming Anchorage had anything remotely resembling traffic.

The aircraft sat on the pad, doors open. A stocky, bearded man stood beside it, looking large enough to fill it entirely himself. Little backward opening doors on either side gave access to a backseat barely worthy of the name. On the grass strip that ran between the tarmac and the landing pad, a gray brown mutt nosed around, which pretty much said all she needed to know about the professionalism of the operation.

"This is Buck," Amy said.

"Y'all ready to fly?" He nodded at the helicopter.

"In there?" Larkin asked faintly. "Are you sure we're all going to fit?" The backseat looked barely wide enough to accommodate two people, let alone three.

He winked. "You'll get to know each other up close and personal."

Larkin glanced over to see Carter and Molly.

And Christopher.

Up close and personal.

"Molly, do you want the front seat?" Carter asked.

"Nope." Buck shook his head. "That's where Scout rides." He whistled, and the dog—more of a hound, really—came loping over, tongue out and a big doggy grin on his face.

"No." Stubbornness glimmered in Carter's eyes. "The front seat is for one of us. The dog stays here."

"Nope," Buck said genially. "Scout always flies with

me. If you want to go, he goes, up front. Unless you want him in the backseat with all of you," he added.

Molly laughed and bent over to rub Scout's ears. "I don't mind giving him the front seat. A flight over the glaciers with a big old dog, now that's an adventure," she said. "Look at this harness you've got, boy. You're all dressed up and ready to go."

Amy gave a pained smile. "Buck is helping us out here, sir. It's the only way we can get you up to the glaciers."

"We're here," Christopher said. "I'd say give it a try."

"If you're not completely happy with the excursion," Amy added, "we'll refund your money."

"We'll see," Carter grumbled, but he was watching Molly make friends with Scout, who seemed very close to being in love.

Larkin only wished she was feeling so good about it. "I'll stay here. All four of us can't possibly squeeze into that backseat. There's no room."

Buck looked them over. "Sure there is. None of you's too wide. It'll just be cozy. Hop in."

Cozy. Exactly what Larkin wanted. She heard a smothered laugh and glanced over to see Christopher watching her.

"I'll take the inside seat. You have the window," Carter told Molly.

"Of course not. You were the one who paid for the trip. You should sit by the window."

"I'm taller than you are," he argued. "You sit on the inside, you won't see a thing. Take the window."

Molly folded her arms. "Only if you take it on the way back."

"You drive a hard bargain."

"Get used to it," she returned.

He considered. "I guess I'll have to."

Christopher glanced over at Larkin. "I'll give you the

window seat, too," he told her. "Just to show you chivalry's alive and well in Alaska."

"Gee, I'm so relieved." She watched him fold his long body into the small space and looked at the postage-stamp patch of seat that remained. Right next to the door.

"Need a hand?" Christopher asked.

"I can do it myself." Reluctantly, she raised a clunky boot to the threshold of the cabin, hoisting herself in and settling back into the alarmingly small space. There was no way to do it halfway. Even staying as close to the edge as she could, she was still unable to keep from touching Christopher.

"All right, over all the way," Buck ordered. "I gotta shut the door."

She wasn't about to look at Christopher and see the humor that she knew would be dancing in his eyes. Instead, she stared studiously ahead and shifted over. Then the little back door slammed and latched with a clunk, leaving her wedged in place.

It was impossible to shut out the awareness of his body. They were practically welded together from ankle to shoulder. It didn't matter that there were layers of clothing between them. What she felt most of all was strength. He might have looked rangy, almost lanky at a glance, but with her body glued up against his, Larkin could feel that he was solid with muscle.

Buck hoisted himself into his seat and whistled. "Scout, load up." Scout hopped up into the helicopter, panting as Buck snapped a pair of chains onto his harness. The pilot put on a bright yellow headset and busied himself for a few moments, checking dials and flicking switches.

He turned to them. "Each of you grab a set of those headphones hanging above you. Once I start the engine, you won't be able to hear a thing unless you got 'em on. It's two-way, so holler if you got a question or want to get a better look at anything." There was a click and the rotors started turning. "Okay, guys, we're ready to go."

Larkin tensed.

Christopher turned to hand her a headset, then gave her a double take. Frowning, he leaned in close as the whine of the motor grew to a roar. "You okay?"

She nodded and tried for a careless smile as the helicopter began to shudder, but it felt more like a grimace.

Because Larkin had a secret. A seasoned traveler she might have been, but she'd never ridden in a helicopter. Jets, yes, Gulfstreams, of course. Even the odd Cessna, they were all fine.

Helicopters scared her silly.

Everybody else seemed totally confident about the ride. As far she was concerned, they were crazy. Something about a helicopter seemed a bit too improbable to really work. After all, straight wings were everywhere you looked in nature—birds, dragonflies, even mosquitoes.

She couldn't think of a single critter that had blades whirling around over its head.

The sound of the motor changed. Larkin stared out the window, feeling panic clog her throat.

Suddenly her fingers were caught up in a strong grip. She looked down to see Christopher's hand clasping hers and glanced up to see him wink.

"We'll be fine," he mouthed at her over the din.

"Okay, folks," Buck said. "Here we go."

And with a bounce, they lifted off into the air.

She'd endure the flight, Larkin told herself grimly, even if she wound up sweat soaked and emotionally exhausted by the end. But as Juneau fell away and the helicopter rose over the ridgeline that ran behind it, an almost giddy magic took hold of her.

She'd had no idea it would be like this. They were surrounded by Plexiglas, but it felt more like really flying, soaring over a snow-covered landscape like a bird. Then ahead of them rose a ridge higher than the rest. And Buck aimed directly for it.

Larkin's heart pounded a little bit, equal parts excitement and nerves. Her grip on Christopher's hand tightened, and she felt him squeeze back. It seemed simply too high for the helicopter to get over, as though they would hook a skid and go tumbling down the mountainside. But instead, with an almost insouciant flick of the control stick, Buck sent them up and over.

And she caught her breath.

The glacier unfurled below them, a long sweep of gray-white snaking between ridgelines, looking almost incongruously smooth amid the rugged landscape. "That's the Taku glacier below us," Buck said. "It's the only one you'll see today that's still growing. All the others are receding."

He sent the aircraft tilting a little bit, edging in toward the ground.

"Oh, *look.*" The words just burst out of her. One minute, they were flying over the striated, dirty gray snow of the glacier. The next, she was staring down into a long crevasse at the most intense, most luminous blue she had ever seen. Impossible to believe such a gorgeous, glowing color existed. She couldn't stop looking at it, turning to glance back as they flew past.

"Can you take us by that again?" someone asked, echoing the words in her head. It was Christopher, she realized.

Larkin glanced over at him quickly to see him watching her, not the glacier. Something flipped in her stomach, something she didn't think had anything at all to do with the motion of the helicopter. Suddenly, it was hard to breathe.

"There's your crevasse." Christopher pointed beyond her. It released her from the spell, and she turned, gulping air. It was just the close confines of the cabin, she told herself. Too many people, not enough air, all of it making her light-headed. That was all.

She stared down at the glacier, amazed at how clearly she could see it. The surface, she realized belatedly, was coming closer. They were dropping, lower and lower still, until, soft as thistledown, the helicopter settled onto the ice.

Chapter Four

"Okay, you got to be smart here," Buck said as the rotors ran down. "Watch yourself on the ice. Even with them boots, you can slip. And be careful around the crevasses. You want to look into 'em, do it from the ends. You do it from the sides and you're gonna get a closer look than you bargained for. And if you fall in, I guarantee Scout and I ain't comin' after you."

Larkin put on her hat and stepped carefully down on the ice. She started to walk a little ways away and turned back to the helicopter, only to see Christopher watching her. "What?"

"Don't let that hat fall off. Scout's likely to think it's a rabbit."

"Don't make fun of this hat. I like this hat."

"I like that hat on you, too. You look like you should be sitting in Red Square drinking Stoli."

She sniffed. "You're lucky there's no loose snow here I could make a snowball from."

"You're from L.A. What would you know about snowballs?"

"Certain things come naturally," she said silkily and walked over toward a fissure on the face of the glacier. She wanted to see that blue, that impossible, luminous pale blue-green that was almost ethereal enough to make her believe in angels.

Circling around, she approached the crevasse from the end, craning her neck to see in. Mostly, she saw the dirty gray-brown ice of the surface. When she got close enough to peer down a bit, she saw a pale blue, but not the glowing color that she craved. There was a little puddle of water on the surface, and her boots splashed she stepped in it. Christopher crunched along behind.

And then, finally, she saw it. It was as though the crevasse were lit from the inside. She feasted her eyes on it, almost hypnotized by the purity of the shade and the glow. "That color is incredible." She exhaled, edging in. "Have you ever seen anything like it? I just want to stare at it for—"

The faint crackle took her by surprise. She'd no more registered it than she felt the ice underfoot begin to give way. The short, sharp scream was ripped out of her throat by pure fear, then cut off as an arm clamped around her ribs and yanked her away. And she and Christopher tumbled back together onto the ice.

It had been like a montage, the crackle of ice, the lurch toward the crevasse and then the fall away, Christopher beneath her, holding her close. For an instant, she just lay against him, cradled in his arms.

Then he released her. "Jesus, are you okay?"

"Fine," she said as she sat up. "Totally fine."

Except for a ferocious case of the shakes.

"What the hell were you trying to do, anyway?" Christopher said roughly, pushing back onto his feet. "You heard Buck. Stay away from the edges. You practically walked right into that thing."

Larkin stared at him, mouth agape. "I did not," she retorted, spine stiffening. "He said look from the ends. I was looking from the end."

"You were almost looking at your end. Next time, stay away from it."

Her chin rose. "Don't tell me what to do."

He held out a hand to her. She ignored it and stood, brushing ice crystals off her coat.

Scout dashed up, barking madly. Behind him crowded Carter and Molly, wide-eyed. "What happened?" Carter demanded.

To cover the fact that her hands were still trembling, Larkin shoved them into her pockets. "Nothing. I, uh—"

"Slipped," Christopher cut in. "She slipped and fell on the ice."

"That was supposed to be my job," Molly said.

Carter shook his head. "These boots aren't as good as they said they were."

"The boots are fine," Larkin said. "I was just clumsy."

"Be careful," Molly said. "Christopher, watch out for her."

"I'm on it," he said.

"I don't need you to watch out for me," Larkin hissed at him as the others walked away.

"Gee, Christopher, thanks for saving my ass."

She flushed. "All right, I appreciate what you did, but I'm not going to take getting yelled at."

"How about if we make a deal? I won't yell at you if you promise you'll stop trying to walk into crevasses."

"I wasn't trying to walk into a crevasse," she retorted.

"And I wasn't trying to yell at you," he snapped, dragging off his hat. Taking a long, deep breath, he scrubbed at his hair, then exhaled slowly. "Look, I'm sorry if I sounded ticked off. Just be careful, okay? You about took ten years off my life back there."

Her hands weren't the only ones that were shaking, Larkin realized, watching him. She nodded slowly.

"I'm sorry I scared you," she said. "You're right. You did save my ass."

The corners of his mouth tugged up. "And a fine ass it is, too. Be a shame to leave it behind on the glacier."

"I'll do my best to watch out for it."

"I'll do my best to keep an eye on it, too."

There was a shout from Buck behind them at the helicopter. "Load up."

Christopher raised his eyebrows. "So are you ready for another helicopter ride, or have you had all the adventure you can take?"

She grinned. "Who, me? I'm just getting started."

The shadows had lengthened by the time the van brought them back to the pier. Across the waterfront boulevard lay ranks of shops catering to the tourist trade, from stores selling jewelry and gifts to the Harley-Davidson store with Juneau T-shirts in the window.

Christopher turned to Carter and shook his hand. "Thanks for letting us come along."

"What a wonderful day." Molly beamed. "Thank you so much, Carter. It was lovely."

"My pleasure." Carter glanced at his watch, and then back at Molly. "The ship doesn't sail for hours yet. Can I interest you in exploring Juneau a little bit?"

He held out his arm, and after a moment's hesitation, she took it.

Christopher watched them walk away and turned back to Larkin. "What about you? You going to go back on board or wander around Juneau for a while? I was thinking about taking the tram up Mount Roberts."

"The tram?" She craned her neck to see the little red car working its way up the mountain.

"What you say? It's not nearly as scary as the helicopter."

She raised her chin. "That helicopter didn't bother me a bit."

"So I noticed. Good thing. It sure spooked me. I was glad you held my hand when we took off."

Her lips twitched. "I'm happy to do whatever I can for you."

He caught at her hand and brought it to his mouth. "I appreciate that," he murmured against her skin. "Remind me to give you a list later."

He looked up at her, eyes dark, and Larkin felt the sharp punch of desire.

"So what's it going to be, the tram or the ship?"

She moistened her lips. "The tram," she managed. If they went back to one of their cabins, she had a pretty good feeling they'd never leave.

"Oh, this is lovely." The boutique was more gallery than shop, with necklaces of beaten gold and topaz lying side by side with handmade Inuit dolls. The walls were a warm tan, the carpet plush and everything gleamed under the overhead track lighting.

Molly stood before a display of Swarovski crystal, fingering a stylized polar bear.

"Is walking through a gift shop like a busman's holiday for you?" Carter watched her. "It probably just makes you think of your place, doesn't it?"

Molly laughed and turned toward the door. "Hardly. Our shop is nothing like this. It's small, more crafts and food than artsy stuff. Comfortable, not upscale," she elaborated as they walked back out into the chill sunshine.

"Then it fits you."

"Are you saying I'm not upscale?" she asked mischievously.

"I'm saying you're more at ease with yourself than about anyone I can think of."

A moment passed by and a smile bloomed over her face. "That might very well be one of the nicest compliments I've ever gotten."

"Then you obviously haven't been hanging around the right people," he said. "I can think of a whole lot of nice compliments to give to you."

"Oh, you." Suddenly bashful, she made a show of staring into a shop window.

On the sidewalk in front of a T-shirt shop, they passed a little novelty machine that promised to impress a scene of Juneau on a penny. Carter stopped and fished out some coins. "Okay, what should I get?"

Molly studied the images. "The glacier, of course. A memento of your day."

He fed the coins in and turned the handle, and with a clink, the flattened penny fell into the slot. He fished it out and handed it to her. "A memento of your day."

"That's yours."

"And now it's yours. Consider it a Valentine's Day present."

She frowned. "It's not Valentine's Day, you silly man," she said.

"Oh, yeah? I guess you'll just have to keep it until it is."

* * *

"It looks so different from up here," Larkin murmured. They leaned on the rail of the Mount Roberts observation platform, staring down at the port spread out beneath them. The cruise ships at the pier looked like toy boats on a play sea, the streets of Juneau stretching out beyond. "It's bigger than I thought it was."

Christopher nodded, leaning against the rail beside her. "Perspective has a way of changing everything."

The slopes around them were closely furred with evergreens, some of them close enough to touch. Even in August, patches of ice and snow still covered the ground. Overhead, a bird that might have been a sort of hawk circled, studying the landscape below.

"I wonder what it's like to live someplace this gorgeous."

"Cold, I imagine," Christopher said.

She pushed at his shoulder. "Seriously. You wake up in the morning and this is outside your door."

"I expect it's like anything else," he said, straightening. "Ninety percent of the time, they probably don't really see it. They're too busy worrying about the grocery shopping or Johnny's grades or the weird noise their car has started making. But every year I bet there are a few days when they walk outside and look around and say, 'Good Lord, we live in paradise.' I hope it happens more for them than it does for most people."

She tilted her head. "I wouldn't have picked you for a cynic."

"Not a cynic, a realist. I imagine that's how it works for just about everybody. Maybe not Buddhist monks or whatever, because they make a vocation out of staying in the moment, but pretty much the rest of us, yeah. You ask me, if you've got a life where whenever you think about it, you can say, 'Wow, this is incredible,' you've won the jackpot. Then happiness is just a matter of remembering to pay attention."

"Is that why you left Washington?" she asked. "Because it didn't have the wow factor?"

He moved his shoulders. "The funny thing is, it did at first. I'd be walking through the Senate office building or standing at a reception talking to the Speaker of the House and I'd just get chills, knowing I was that close to the center of everything." He watched the hawk for a moment. "And then one day it stopped seeming like the center of everything and started seeming like the center of not very much at all. I kept trying to do the same stuff over and over and not getting it accomplished, or worse, accomplishing stuff I didn't believe in because it was what I was paid to do."

She studied him. "So what was the breaking point?"

"I went up to Vermont to see my folks for a few days. I stopped by to see Aunt Molly and Jacob. I remember walking outside while the sun was coming up and I just knew there and then I didn't want Washington anymore. I was done. A month and a half later, I bought the farm."

"And does it make you say wow?"

His eyes glimmered with humor. "When I take time to pay attention."

"Shame on you."

"I'm human, just like the people who live here."

The platform had cleared out so that they were the only ones left. After being on the ship with so many people, there was something soothing about having space to themselves.

Larkin looked out over the streets of Juneau. "It must be strange to be locked in here."

"What do you mean?"

"Didn't you read? There aren't any roads out of town. You can't get here by car, only ship or plane. Now there's a trade-off—you live in paradise but you can't escape."

"I imagine it would get old after a while."

"It did for Adam and Eve. I think I'd rather have an imperfect place," she decided as they crossed to the other side of the deck. "Perfection's boring. What about you?"

"Paradise." His teeth gleamed. "I'd build a road."

When his life hadn't suited him, he'd walked away to make a better one. Not a search for paradise so much as possibility.

She bent to pick up a little twig with a bunch of pine needles at the end. "What do they do when they just get a wild hair to go?" she wondered, twirling the needles between her fingers. "I mean, I know if I wake up in the middle of the night and I can't sleep, I can get in the car and just drive, wind up in the desert or the mountains. Keep going and hit Canada, if I want. Or Vermont." Her smile flashed.

He crossed behind her. "You ever wind up in Vermont, stop in and see me."

"I'll do that."

"So do you drive at night a lot?"

"Sometimes. When I'm restless." She turned to face him, found him closer than she'd expected. "Sometimes I wake up and, I don't know…it's like there's something missing, but I can't really put my finger on what it is. So I drive." She shrugged, embarrassed. "That probably sounds nuts. Does it ever happen to you? Do you ever find yourself just wanting something?"

"I want," he murmured. "I want all the time, all of a sudden." He captured her hand in his, took the twig. "But I know exactly what I want."

Larkin swallowed. "What?" she whispered.

"I think you know." He stroked the soft sides of the smooth, pliant needles down her throat. Goose bumps rose in their wake. Watching her, he brought it up to touch along her jaw, over her cheeks.

Larkin's breath shuddered out. She licked her lips, waiting. Never breaking their gaze, he tossed the twig away.

Then she slid her hand around the nape of his neck and pulled him to her.

This time, she would run the show, she thought as her mouth fused to his. She wouldn't find herself weak at his kisses because she'd be the aggressor, taking it deep, moving against him, running her fingers through his hair. It would take away the mystery, take away the fascination, and he'd be just another man.

Except then he began to kiss her back, and he wasn't just another man at all.

She thought she knew what to expect. After all, they'd kissed before. She knew about the hot rush of need in her veins, the tease, the temptation. How was it that he found new ways to overwhelm her senses, new ways to send desire flowing through her, hot and thick and undeniable? How was it that in trying to seduce, she found herself the one most truly losing control?

His hands slipped inside her open coat, drawing her against him, sliding over her curves until she moaned into his mouth. Barriers, there were always barriers between them. And yet it felt as though the caress of lips upon lips, tongue upon tongue, went deeper than surface touch, striking some chord deep within her.

It was dizzying. Larkin knew she was on solid ground. She knew there was a rail behind her; yet it felt like she was poised to fall from some high precipice, like the twig he'd tossed away. His touch was mesmerizing, his taste dizzying. With all the world spread out below them, everything had reduced to just this one point in space and time.

Christopher groaned. Desire was a physical ache that ground through him. Every atom in his body cried out for release. He fought the urge to take, to conquer, to satisfy the demand that become a near constant companion in the past two days. He pressed his lips to the taut skin of Larkin's throat, smelling her scent over the sharpness of pine, intoxicating himself with the beckoning warmth and sweetness. He heard the soft intake of her breath, the even softer moan, and pressed her more tightly to him.

In the distance were voices, filtering down from the enclosed walkway overhead that led to the tram terminal. Slowly, torturously, he brought himself under control. There will be a time for them. There would be a place. This was not it. But it was coming—and soon.

In time with his thoughts, there was a clunk above them as the tram docked. "Last trip for the *Alaskan Voyager,* folks," a voice called.

Stepping away from her was the hardest thing he'd ever done.

"We should get back down the mountain, back to the ship," Larkin said unsteadily.

Christopher nodded. "We wouldn't want to get stuck in paradise." He'd take imperfect with Larkin any day.

Chapter Five

Larkin struck the match and watched it flame, then lowered it to light the red candle that stuck out of the blueberry muffin before her. She picked it up and turned toward the veranda where Carter sat out in the cool morning air. Clearing her throat, she broke into a chorus of "Happy Birthday."

"What the…" He turned from his seat at the table, laughing aloud as he caught sight of the candle.

"Happy birthday, dear Dad, happy birthday to you," Larkin sang as she set the muffin next to the remains of their breakfast plates. "And many more." She handed him his flute of champagne and clinked her glass against his. "Now make your wish."

"Yes, ma'am." With a smile of genuine pleasure, he blew out the candle, then took a swallow of champagne. They sat in the sun, the snowy fjords of Glacier Bay moving majestically past. "I've got to give you credit, you went all out," Carter said. "Not just breakfast but a birthday cake."

"Nothing but the best for you." She raised her glass again. "Here's to the end of the first half and the start of the second."

"The first half?" he repeated. "You're expecting me to live to a hundred and twenty?"

Larkin took a sip of champagne and let the bubbles pop against her teeth. "I'm hoping so. It would bode well for me."

"I'll tell you one thing, I'm sure as hell not going to make it if I keep having breakfasts like this." Unrepentantly, Carter crunched on his last piece of bacon.

"It's your birthday. Nothing you eat all day has any calories or any cholesterol. It's a rule."

"In that case, call room service and have them bring me a ribeye with a baked potato and all the fixings."

"Nope, that's for dinner. We've got reservations at eight."

"Running my life, now, are you?"

"Someone has to, and your assistant's back in New York. I'm rising to the occasion," she told him.

The smile faded but stayed in Carter's eyes as he looked at her. "Thanks for coming."

"Thanks for having me," Larkin returned lightly.

"I'm glad you're here." He reached out and squeezed her shoulder. "Are you enjoying yourself?"

"Of course, lots," she said. "How about you?"

"Yes." He gave her a sidelong glance. "Except for a few notable exceptions."

Larkin's lips twitched. "You didn't have to go on the zip line," she said. "I told you I could do it alone."

"No little girl of mine is going to do some damn fool death-defying stunt without me following right after her like an idiot," he said.

"You're an inspiration to us all."

It felt like old times, when things had been good between them. Perhaps she'd been a little disappointed to see

Carter dive headlong into another crush, but in a way Molly Trask and her family had provided the initial buffer that had allowed the two of them to get comfortable with one another again. That was what counted.

Who cared if she hadn't seen hide nor hair of Christopher Trask since they'd left Juneau?

"So what have we got today?" Carter asked.

She pulled out the ship's daily newspaper that she'd pulled from the clip outside her door. "Let's see, we're on the ship all day, cruising the bay and looking at glaciers."

"No death-defying stunts?"

"No death-defying stunts," she assured him.

He grinned at her and stood. "It looks like we're slowing down. Let's go get a good spot to see the goods."

Larkin slipped on her coat and slung her scarf around her neck.

"Ready to go?"

She nodded.

The hallway was crowded, a sense of palpable excitement in the air as passengers flowed toward the elevators. The ports were entertaining, but the glaciers were the heart of an Alaskan cruise, and everybody seemed bent on getting to the best possible viewing spot.

Larkin and Carter moved down the hall with the flow. She pulled out her BlackBerry to check messages, turning the corner to the elevator lobby only to run smack into a mob of Trasks.

Including Christopher.

She felt the little surge of butterflies despite herself. There was nothing to get excited about. He'd gone from Casanova to the Invisible Man—it wasn't like she was expecting a whole lot. Not that he owed her anything, of course. He was on a trip with his family, after all; it made sense that he'd spend time with them, just like she'd spent time with Carter. So what if it felt like something had started in Juneau. And then he'd just disappeared, making it seem like it hadn't mattered to him a bit. Par for the course. *That was all right, it didn't matter to her either,* she thought, chin rising.

"Look who's here," he said. "Small world."

"Small ship," she said coolly. She didn't bother to look for Carter; she had a pretty good idea he'd be moving to Molly's side.

"Headed down to watch the glaciers?"

"Along with half the passengers, it looks like."

"Well, it is the main reason most people came."

Jacob looked at the indicator lights over the elevators, which all appeared to be stalled elsewhere. He shook his head impatiently and hoisted up his younger son. "They're never going to get here. Let's just walk."

By general agreement, they all moved toward the broad stairway that led to the other decks. Molly and Carter walked ahead of Larkin, Molly already laughing at some comment or other of Carter's.

A steady tide of passengers streamed down the stairs. Celie caught at the hand of her older son. "Hold on to your uncle Christopher, Sophia," she directed in her lightly accented English.

"I don't need to hold on," Sophia argued.

"Sophia Amelie Trask," Celie said with a crack of warning in her voice.

Jacob turned. "Sophia?"

Recognizing she was beat, Sophia gave in. "Yes, *Maman.*"

Larkin jumped as she felt a little hand slide into hers. She looked down to see Sophia, who gave her a cheeky grin. "You're prettier than my uncle Christopher."

Christopher glanced over at Larkin. "She's right, you know. You are."

She wouldn't be charmed, Larkin told herself.

"So did you have a good time yesterday in port?" Christopher caught at Sophia's other hand so the girl was between them.

"Great."

"Glad to hear it. We weren't so lucky. We were supposed to do one of those rail trips. You know, fly up to Whitehorse and catch the train back? It broke down in the middle of nowhere. We got stranded."

It had Larkin looking at him. "I'm sure that wasn't in the brochure."

"No kidding. We sat there for hours. Almost didn't make it to the pier in time. They were about ready to pull in the gangway when we rolled up."

Sophia jumped from step to step, swinging from their hands.

"It's a good thing you made it back," Larkin said. "Otherwise you'd have missed the best part of the whole trip."

He locked eyes with her. "Don't I know it."

Larkin felt her cheeks heat.

"You're blushing," he said delightedly.

"I am not," she muttered.

"Am, too," Sophia chanted without looking, swinging out to the next step.

"Whose side are you on?" Larkin scolded.

"Uncle Soft Touch's, clearly," Christopher said as they reached the promenade deck. "You already know I'm a soft touch for you," he added, brushing a quick kiss over her lips before they turned to walk outside.

She struggled to ignore the little frisson of excitement that buzzed through her. As with two days before in Juneau, he had a way of making her forget that she was angry with him, or rather, to make the irritation itself seem unwarranted. Now you see him, now you don't, she reminded herself, and turned to the outdoors, to the glaciers. That was why they'd all come, after all.

It might have been August, but their breath formed white plumes in the cold air. A light breeze tossed around strands of hair that had escaped from Larkin's ponytail. The *Voyager* sat dead in the water, facing the end of the glacier, a wall of ice hundreds of feet high. Even across almost half a mile of open water, they could hear the snaps and groans that reminded them that the ice wasn't static but creeping along like some live thing, unyielding, unrelenting, grinding down everything in its quest to reach the water.

Nearly all the passengers on the ship had turned out for the spectacle, seemingly ninety percent of them clustered on the promenade deck. Sophia wormed her way up to the rail to stand next to Celie and Adam. Jacob stood behind with Gerard up on his shoulders.

Molly and Carter stayed back from the crowd, content to watch at a distance.

Larkin glanced at the people clustered three deep at the rail, and then at Christopher. "Ideas?"

He nodded his head toward the stern. "Let's go down there. There aren't so many people. It'll be easier for you to take a couple of 'em down and get their spots."

She raised a brow. "Me?"

"You're the one who was boasting about your *American Gladiators* moves."

"I'll see what I can do," she said dryly.

"That's my girl."

There was something, Larkin thought a moment later, about being at the rail where they could look out with no one in the way. It let them concentrate entirely on the view as the minutes went by and they waited for the glacier to calve.

And what a view.

There weren't enough words in the English language. Beautiful, incredible, amazing, awe-inspiring. They'd all been used, and to describe far less singular sights than what they now stared out at. Millions of years before, an ice sheet had covered the region, flowing under its own weight, relentlessly carving out the fjords they'd been sailing past all morning. Now, the uncovered landscape and remaining glaciers were a study in contrasts: steep rock walls and flat blue water, black-brown stone and pale ice.

Seen edge on, the glacier looked crumpled and torn asunder by powerful, inexorable forces. The jagged face rose above the berg-dotted water, the ice fractured into tilted, jumbled white columns like the teeth of some giant predator. Even the white held a faint hint of cerulean, and in the fissures she caught glimpses of that gorgeous, luminous blue. Across the bottom threaded sinuous lines of gray-black where uncounted years before the glacier had devoured the earth and stone before it, scraping it, compressing it and assimilating it until it became just another stratified layer of ice.

A sharp crack made Larkin jump, the sound carrying clearly in the icy, still air. A flurry of snaps followed. For long moments, nothing happened. Then, with ponderous slowness, an enormous slab of the front face separated away. One instant, it hung there. The next, it began to slip ever faster, pirouetting loose and sliding down. When it slipped into the bay, water geysered up around it. A cluster of seagulls darted in, shrieking and diving at the water to get the fish that had been stunned by the berg that now bobbed at the glacier's base.

"You know, if more people could see things like this, there'd be a lot less call for shoot-'em-up video games," Larkin murmured.

"No, we'd just have video games about shooting icebergs to pieces."

"Cynic." She flicked him a glance.

"Realist," he countered.

"At least if people could see what we're losing, they'd try harder to cut their carbon footprints."

"The irony of course being that the only way to see Glacier Bay is from the water, so anyone who's not kayaking in is blowing their carbon footprint all to hell. But I do agree, it's quite a show." He leaned against the rail beside her.

"Just imagine, the captain and crew get to see it every week."

"I'd guess they don't really bother to look. It's probably old hat to them by now."

"Cynic."

His lips twitched. "Realist."

"Some things you don't ever get tired of looking at."

"No," he agreed, but when she glanced over he was watching her.

Her mouth went dry. "You're not looking at the glacier."

"No," he said again. "I missed seeing you yesterday."

Something fluttered in her stomach. "That's what you get for picking a broken-down train."

"I know, and I was punished for it. Have dinner with me."

He was side by side with her, his elbow on the rail almost touching hers. She couldn't stop staring at his mouth. She moistened her lips. "I can't. It's Carter's birthday. We've got plans."

"The whole night?" He reached over to tuck a loose strand of hair behind her ear. His touch lingered on her cheek for a few seconds, completely derailing her thought processes.

"What are you doing?" she asked.

"Thinking about kissing you. I've been thinking about it a lot."

He ran his fingertips over her jaw and down her throat, leaving a trail of warmth. It had her muscles softening. It had her wanting more.

"Maybe you should loosen this scarf," he suggested.

It took work to steady her voice. "There are people all around us."

"They're all looking at the glacier," he told her, nipping at her lip. "Your mouth drives me crazy, you know. Kiss me."

"We can't."

"We can." Swiftly, he caught at her wrist and led her a few yards down the deck to where it cut across the superstructure of the ship. He pressed her against the wall of the deserted tunnel and with an almost desperate hunger, fused his mouth to hers.

There was the connection, there was the sparring, but at the foundation of it all was this, this white-hot need that burned in them both. All around them was ice. Here, in the shelter of the tunnel, there was only heat.

It was foolish. It was heedless. Christopher knew they had no business taking such a chance, and yet somehow he couldn't make himself care. He dove his hands into the silken mass of her hair, drawing her head back to feast on her throat, pressing his lips to where her pulse beat frantically below the skin.

The wanting drummed through him, as it had during the hours of the previous night, as it had the whole day before. Now, feeling her body soft and yielding against his, all he wanted was more.

They were in public, their families just around the corner. Anyone might walk up at any time. It should have mattered.

It didn't.

It would have terrified her if she'd been thinking rationally. Larkin had kissed plenty of men, but none of them had ever been able to make her lose control. Now, she couldn't think for the inferno, couldn't speak, couldn't do anything but feel. His mouth demanded, his hands took. When her lips shuddered apart, he dipped in to taste and in that one swift move stripped her emotions down to naked desire and fundamental need.

It would be so easy to go over the edge, Christopher thought hazily, to race with her upstairs to a room and find oblivion. He couldn't, though, he knew. They couldn't. They had family; they had obligations. Between the two of them, there was only desire, and it fell way down on the list of priorities.

Except he had the uneasy feeling it wasn't as simple as that. There was something about the two of them together that made him greedy for more: not just more of that tempting mouth, that deliciously curved body, but more of her. More time, all the time they could manage, even though the clock rolled relentlessly, taking them faster and faster toward the day they'd dock in Vancouver and say goodbye.

He knew it, but even as every fiber of him shuddered to go forward, he made himself pull back. He watched her eyes open, watched the passion fade and common sense take over.

She took an uneven breath. "We should…"

"Get back out to watch the glacier," he finished. They walked out of the tunnel, the cool air helping clear his head.

"We're moving again," Larkin said slowly. "That means we're going to the next glacier. We should go back."

"I still want to see you."

She raised her fingers to her lips almost absently. "It's Carter's birthday. I want to spend as much of it with him as he wants."

Christopher nodded. "Fair enough. What about before?"

"We're going to the captain's reception."

"So are we. But what about just the two of us?"

"We could meet before the reception," she offered. "If I know Carter, he'll want to spend at least a little bit of time with your aunt."

"If he wants to do that, he'll have to take the group package. We've got plans."

"I guess we're out of luck, then."

"Not necessarily. You could come along."

"What is it?"

He grinned. "Trust me. You'll love it."

Chapter Six

"Bingo?" Larkin stared at the electronic number board in the ship's theater.

"Don't tell me you've never played. Nobody's that sophisticated."

"In nursery school, I think. It hasn't exactly been a big part of my entertainment world."

Christopher smiled. "Come on, add a little excitement to your life."

"I'm not sure the words *bingo* and *excitement* belong in the same sentence."

"Sure they do," he said. "It's just how you play. We could have a little side bet. Say, if I get more matches than you do, you have to go out with me to the top deck for that drink."

"I bought you a drink in Juneau before we went up on the tram."

"Oh, no. That was you thanking me for saving your, ah—" he glanced at Keegan and Kelsey "—neck. Okay, how about this? For the rest of the cruise, you have to give up your CrackBerry."

"My BlackBerry?" She blanched. "I can't do that. I might get work e-mail."

"Are you a neurosurgeon? Would it be a matter of life or death?"

"Well, no, but—"

"It's only today and tomorrow. Give it up. It'll be good for what ails you."

As though it were aware it was being talked about, her BlackBerry gave a peremptory low-power bleat. Larkin glanced down at her pocket.

"Battery running down?" Christopher asked. At her nod, he looked satisfied. "Okay, here's what we do. If I win, you let it run down completely and you give me your battery charger."

"What?" she yelped.

"Relax, I'll give it back to you the day we land back in port. If you win, I—"

"Take Sophia and her brothers for a walk around the deck."

"Sophia?" he replied plaintively.

"And her brothers."

He gave her a quick look. "All right, whatever you say."

Larkin eyed him. "Why do I get the feeling you've got this rigged somehow?"

"Rigged? Me? Hardly. You're just afraid to say yes because you know I'll win."

She sniffed. "Bring it on, big boy."

"You're on."

The theater looked like a stylized Egyptian temple as interpreted by Tiffany, all pillars and colored metal panels separated by black lines. At the front, staffers sold bingo cards. And in the seats were a surprising number of players.

Predictably, the Trasks commandeered a pair of long couches at the back wall of the theater. Carter brought over a chair for Molly.

"Okay," said Hadley, handing around bingo cards. "Whoever wins is buying dinner."

"Uh, we're on a cruise, sweetheart. Dinner's free," Gabe reminded her.

She settled beside him, eyes dancing. "Well, then, it should be easy."

"What pattern are we trying for?" asked Christopher's sister Lainie.

"A check mark," Hadley replied. "The prize is a facial at the spa."

"A facial?" Lainie repeated.

"Back off, babe. This one's for me."

"You want it, sweet pea?" Lainie shot back. "You're gonna have to take me down first."

Hadley looked at J.J. "Okay by you?"

He smiled broadly. "As long as I get to watch."

"Make that two of us," Gabe put in. "And can you add a little baby oil?"

"Behave yourselves!" Molly scolded. "Honestly, anyone would think you boys were still in junior high."

"Wait a minute, what did I do?" Christopher asked aggrievedly.

"Sssshh," Celie hissed, "the game's starting."

"Okay, everyone, the first ball is the vitamin ball," the emcee said, "B 12. That's B 12."

"One for me." Christopher poked through the tab on his card then leaned over to look at Larkin's. "Got it?"

"Nope," she said.

"Bummer. You get the center one for free, you know."

It wasn't part of the check mark pattern. She glowered at him. "Thanks for your help."

"Think nothing of it."

"N 45," the emcee said. "N 45."

Christopher punched another spot.

"O 63, O 63."

Christopher glanced over at her card. "How you making out?"

"None of your business," Larkin said, shielding her card.

"You haven't gotten any yet?"

"Pay attention to your own game." She nudged him away.

"Okay, now we've got N 50," said the emcee. "That's N 50, the Snow White ball."

"Snow White ball?" Larkin asked, puzzled.

"Five oh, five oh, it's off to work we go," Christopher said in a singsong voice.

"B 6, that's B 6."

"I had no idea you were such a bingo hound," Larkin said, checking her card a second time to be sure she didn't have it.

He shrugged. "They do fund-raiser games at Sophia and Adam's school. I play every year."

She folded her arms. "So you're telling me I got fished in by a bingo hustler."

"You agreed to the bet. No backing out now."

Larkin snorted.

"G 38," said the emcee, "G 38."

"Finally," Larkin said, punching her card.

Christopher glanced over. "Hey, you got one. Good for you. I mean, too bad you're three behind but it's a start."

"Eat hot death," she said.

"I 24, I 24."

"Bingo!" someone shouted.

Christopher looked over at her card with its lonely little bent tab and his own. Then he reached down and punched I 24. "Hey, look at that. I guess that means I win."

Larkin scowled. "You rigged this."

"How could I have rigged this?"

"I don't know. Maybe you slipped a twenty to the emcee."

"Nope. Face it, Hayes, you lost."

Larkin thought a minute. "Two out of three?"

"And you thought bingo would be boring."

"Okay, next game," the emcee announced. "This will be on your blue card, your blue card, and the shape is an X. Ready? Let's go."

Larkin had hung out at the hippest clubs on three continents. She'd walked down runways in Paris, Milan and New York. But as she sat in a cruise ship lounge playing bingo with a predominantly over-sixty crowd, to her eternal surprise, she had fun. Maybe it was the rapid-fire stream of jokes and jabs that the Trask clan traded. Maybe it was the bad puns of the emcee. Maybe it was just sitting next to Christopher. Somehow, it was the fastest hour she'd ever been through, even if she only had a couple of matches on the last—and biggest—game. It didn't matter. It didn't matter because...

"Bingo!"

Larkin looked over to see Molly Trask on her feet waving her card ebulliently.

"So what are you going to do with your big score?" Carter asked. He and Molly sat in the arcade watching the grandkids play Ping-Pong.

"My five hundred thirty-seven dollars?" Molly looked at him in amusement. "Oh, I don't know. Buy presents for the grandkids with some of it, I suppose. Maybe really splurge and frame a needlepoint scene my grandmother made when I was a girl."

"Not going to save it for another cruise? Spend a day in Vancouver?"

"I don't think so. It's been fun, but I need to get back. I miss the store, I miss home." She gave an embarrassed shrug. "I guess I'm not cut out for fancy stuff."

Carter shook his head. "I wish I liked my life as much as you do," he said.

She turned to him. "A man as successful as you? I find that hard to believe."

The Ping-Pong ball bounced off the table and rolled to their feet. Carter picked it up and tossed it back to Adam. "What's success, racking up zeros or being happy with yourself? After a while, success stops meaning anything. It kind of becomes a habit. Doing for the sake of doing."

"Doing for the sake of doing could describe all of us sooner or later."

"Yeah? Does it describe you? Do you do just for the sake of doing?"

The tone of his voice had her looking at him. "Yes and no," she said slowly. "I don't look at it as just getting along, if that's what you mean. To me, the day-to-day things are what matter. Making dinner, gardening, hanging up wash. It's like, I don't know…maybe my own way of praying."

He stared at her.

"What?" she said, flushing.

"And you still don't think there's anything special about your life? Molly Trask, you are one in a million."

"Which means there are a couple thousand people just like me in China," she said dryly.

"Lucky me you're the one who's here."

"Now this is my idea of a reception." Lainie dipped a marshmallow happily into the chocolate fountain.

Larkin looked on in amusement. The group of them stood in the glassed-in concierge lounge for the luxury suites, at the captain's reception. The lounge had the feel of some Victorian library or gentlemen's club, all polished mahogany and green shaded lamps, with lighted shelves of magazines and comfortable leather club chairs.

Lainie hummed in pleasure. "Oh, Lord, those strawberries are the best. Although you know what would be even better?" she added thoughtfully. "Chocolate-dipped Doritos."

Celie swallowed. "You're sick."

"No, really," Lainie insisted. "It would be like yogurt-dipped pretzels, sweet and salty."

"Not to mention disgusting," Christopher added, glancing at his brother-in-law. "Did you know she was this eccentric when you met her?"

J.J. took a swallow of his beer. "Life with Lainie has been a journey of constant discovery."

"Oh, come on, Speed, you knew it all the time. That's why you adore me," Lainie said.

"You're right, that's why I do." He leaned in to kiss her. "But it's still disgusting."

"Can I take pictures of you all?" The ship's photographer, a perky redhead, stood before them, camera in hand.

Gabe gave her a pitying look. "I don't know? How much time you got?"

"Girl shot," Lainie proclaimed, slinging her arms around the necks of Hadley and Larkin.

"Hey," Celie complained, edging over with Molly, "we get to be in it, too."

The camera flashed and the photographer glanced around. "Next," she said, lining up Gabe's family, then Jacob's family, then one set of kids, the whole collection, and Lainie and J.J.

"Us," Christopher said, slipping his arm around Larkin. She turned to grin at him, catching the flash on the camera out of the corner of her eye.

"Whoops, sorry," she said. "You'll have to dump that one."

The photographer squinted at the camera. "Actually, it's pretty cute, but I'll take another one just to be sure."

She snapped a shot of Carter and Molly and then glanced around. "Anybody else?"

"Get the two of us." Carter moved next to Larkin. They smiled into the lens together as the camera flashed.

Hadley snapped her fingers. "That's where I know you from," she said suddenly.

Larkin glanced over, slipping away from Carter. "What?"

"*Vanity Fair.* You model, right? I've been racking my brains ever since we met, trying to figure out why you looked so familiar. I read about you in that article with Ivanka Trump and the Gettys. They had an old picture of you with your dad."

"Oh, that," she said, embarrassed.

Christopher stared at her. "You're a model?"

"Not full-time. It's just something I do." Larkin never quite knew how to respond when people brought up her modeling. She always felt like a bit of a fraud. It wasn't a real job, just something that had cropped up because of who she was and who she knew. Like everything about her life, it wasn't something she'd made happen.

"I guess you do have a glamour job after all," Christopher said slowly.

"Well, it's not *American Gladiators.*"

"No," he agreed. "It's not."

One of the benefits of spending more than eleven years as a lobbyist was that Christopher had gotten really good at going through receptions on autopilot. The key, a long-ago mentor had taught him, was to watch body language and smile and nod at the right moment. It had allowed him many a time to calculate strategy for persuading one congressional member while talking to another.

Now, he found himself flipping on autopilot again, only partially tuning in to the conversation at hand. Mostly so that he could focus on Larkin.

Only five days had passed since the two of them had met. It was ludicrous to think that he knew her at all.

He still felt blindsided.

A model, just like his ex-wife. *I married for the sweet smell of success, not the stink of a goat herd.* The scathing words played over in his head. Nicole had been obsessed with three things: parties, her BlackBerry and money. So far, what he knew about Larkin was that she was from L.A., hung out at parties and seemed to have her Black-Berry out every five minutes.

Just like Nicole.

How had he missed that? Somehow, they'd clicked, and on the strength of that, he'd deluded himself into thinking that Larkin was someone different than who she was. He'd come three thousand miles to meet a woman he couldn't get out of his head, only to find out she was just like the one he'd already divorced. The one who'd divorced him.

Fate had a sick sense of humor.

Larkin leaned in to him. "Everything okay?"

"Yeah, sure," he said. He looked at her mouth, and he could still taste her, still feel her against him.

"I need to get going so that I can get ready for dinner," Larkin said.

"I'll see you later, then."

"Aren't you forgetting something?"

"What?"

"The charger for my BlackBerry. After all, you did win the bet."

He studied her. "Are you sure you can do without your BlackBerry for two days?"

"Weren't you the one who was telling me I should learn to?" she asked.

"I suppose, but that was before I knew what you did. Kind of hard for you to go off the grid, I imagine."

"Carter always told me never to make a bet I couldn't afford to lose," she said.

"I guess that means you owe me a charger, then."

Christopher had just finished shaving for dinner when the knock came. He wiped off the shaving cream but didn't bother to put on a shirt. He opened the door to find Jacob.

"Sorry, I didn't mean to interrupt."

"Hey, no problem. Come on in."

Jacob's height and broad shoulders dwarfed the narrow entrance hall. He was a man built for the outdoors, not for postage-stamp rooms. He was already dressed for dinner, managing to look both stylish and remarkably uncomfortable.

"Grab a seat," Christopher said. He walked over to the closet and drew out a pale blue shirt. "What's up?"

Jacob perched on the couch, making it look ridiculously small. He looked at his hands. "Maybe nothing. Celie says I'm nuts."

"Hell, I could've told you that."

Jacob glowered at him from under his brows. "You know anything about this Hayes guy?"

Christopher stopped in the middle of buttoning his shirt. "You mean Carter Hayes?"

Jacob nodded. "The guy's been underfoot this whole trip."

Christopher suppressed a smile. The man was a billionaire, and Jacob talked about him like he was a pesky gnat. "Your mom seems pretty taken with him."

"That's kind of the problem. He just came in here and swept her off her feet."

It was all Christopher could do not to laugh. The words *swept her off her feet* sounded so absurd coming from Jacob, and he couldn't think of anyone less likely to be swept than the ever-practical Molly. And yet…

And yet she'd had a sparkle in her eyes the past few days that he hadn't seen for a decade.

He should have noticed; he should have thought about it. Instead, he'd been preoccupied with Larkin.

"Mom hasn't really…dated since Dad died. And now, here's this slick operator, putting the moves on her. She's not used to it. And we don't know a damned thing about him." It was the next best thing to a soliloquy for Jacob.

"That slick operator is worth a couple billion dollars, or at least he was when I was in Washington and following the industry." Christopher tucked in his shirt. "It's probably more now."

Jacob blinked. "Yeah. Well. Anything else?"

"No legal scandals." Christopher flipped up his collar and slung a tie around his neck. "I seem to remember hearing about a couple of divorces. Can't say I know any of the details."

Jacob nodded. "That's the kind of thing I'm talking about. They're not our kind of people."

"So, what, are you looking to go rough him up and tell him to steer clear?"

Jacob gave him a stare. "Funny."

"Jacob, we're on a cruise. Tomorrow we dock in Vancouver. We go home, the Hayeses go home and that's that." And despite everything, it had been driving him nuts.

They're not our kind of people.

He was being an idiot, Christopher decided. So what if she modeled? It wasn't like it signified. She lived in L.A., for Christ's sake. It wasn't like there was any potential for a future anyway. What the hell did it matter if she'd suddenly turned out to be different than he'd thought? What the hell did it matter if she had the same job as his ex-wife?

It was a cruise, not a lifetime commitment. If he were smart, he'd put it out of his head and do his best to burn out this addiction he had for her before they went their separate ways.

If he were smart.

Christopher finished tying his tie and turned to Jacob. "Look, are you sure this is any of our business?"

"I thought maybe you'd take this seriously." Jacob rose.

"I am taking it seriously, Jacob. I get what you're concerned about. I just don't know the best way to handle it." Christopher blew out a breath. "Look, if you want me to talk to her, I'll talk to her."

Jacob looked relieved. "I'd screw it up."

"I may, too."

"I just don't want to see her expect something and then get hurt when all he does is walk away."

All any of them could do was walk away, and if they didn't, they wouldn't be any better off.

That was the hell of it.

Chapter Seven

Carter had always been one to get up early. At home, it didn't present a problem—he'd order breakfast and the paper, turn on his computer and get to work. Aboard ship, he didn't know what to do. It wasn't like he didn't have his laptop and BlackBerry with him, but he had zero interest in turning them on, a situation he found extraordinary, inexplicable and vaguely unsettling.

Which was why he found himself stepping out onto the topmost deck of the ship as the sun was coming up. A walk in the cool morning air might not take care of the queer restlessness that had overtaken him but at least it would keep him busy.

Ahead of him, he saw a familiar figure at the rail. His mouth curved and he approached.

"Molly?"

She started but didn't turn to face him, not right away. When she did, her eyes were red-rimmed.

The concern was immediate. "What's wrong?"

"Nothing," she said quickly.

"It's not nothing. What's happened? Tell me." He stopped beside her. "I can help."

"Oh, Carter." Her voice caught. "There's nothing you can do."

"Of course there is. Tell me what's going on."

Instead, she turned away from him toward the horizon where the sun was just rising over the edge of the mountains. "It's barely four-thirty in the morning. Isn't it extraordinary to have the sun coming up?"

"Molly…" he said.

"I'm just being silly. It's an anniversary." Her hands tightened on the rail. "Ten years ago today, I lost my husband."

Whatever words he'd thought to say died in his throat. Instead, he reached out to set his hand over hers on the rail and let the quiet moments speak for themselves. "I'm sorry," he said finally. "Of all the people I've ever met, you most deserve to be happy."

She exhaled. "I am happy, Carter. It's just that sometimes…" She swallowed. "I miss him."

"I know." His voice was quiet. "It's been fifteen years since Larkin's mother was killed, and sometimes I still feel like I could walk into the other room and find her there."

"It's funny how it hits you. Months at a time will go by and then all of a sudden it'll be like it happened yesterday." Molly wiped her eyes. "Anyway, I'm sorry you saw me. I just had to get it out. The boys brought me on this trip to take my mind off the anniversary. I don't want them to feel bad that it didn't work."

It was so like Molly, always worried about others. Carter smiled. "Your secret's safe with me."

As if by agreement, they moved away from the rail and began to walk. He watched her, still lovely in the sunrise.

"Why haven't you ever remarried?" he asked. "A woman like you…"

Her eyes softened. "You don't get what Adam and I had more than once in a lifetime. I've got the kids and the farm. I keep busy."

"But is it enough?"

"I'm content," she said. "I love my family."

"That's not an answer."

"I'm not sure I have one. Life is different. I miss him every day." She gave an embarrassed smile. "I talk to him sometimes. That's one of the advantages of living alone. You can talk to someone who's not there, and you don't have anybody trying to cart you off to a headshrinker."

Carter stopped at the rail and looked out at the water. "I used to talk to Beth sometimes," he said. "Especially about Larkin. I remember the night after we lost her, just waking up completely panicked, thinking I had this beautiful little girl and absolutely no idea how I was going to raise her alone."

"But you did," Molly said gently. "She's turned into a lovely young woman because of you."

"*Despite* me," he countered. "I was a horse's ass. I couldn't deal with it, being alone, not after the way it had been. I just wanted that feeling back so I married the first woman I felt good around. Idiot," he said bitterly. "Like running out of Wheaties and going to the grocery store to buy a new box. I wanted a mother for Larkin. I wanted a wife. I figured it would work. I just didn't know…" He stared out over the water. "With Beth and me it was like lightning in a bottle. The minute we met, I just knew. We were…"

"I know," Molly said.

"I wasn't smart like you. I didn't realize how rare that was. So I'd meet a woman and get a glimpse of that feeling, and think okay, here it is, I've finally found it again. Except

I never did. But I kept trying, over and over again. And I dragged Larkin along every damn time."

"Don't beat yourself up, Carter. You can't go back and change it. You thought you were doing the right thing." Her words were soft.

"I didn't know what the hell I was doing."

"Well, you must have done something right. She's a daughter to be proud of."

"Whoever she is, I didn't have much to do with it. She's been her own self from the day she was born."

"Aren't they always?" Molly asked.

"I can't believe we forgot to get a present for Rowdy," Lainie told Christopher as they wandered through the Northern Lights boutique in the ship's central shopping gallery. "We got something for Mom, Dad and Daniel."

"The little brother always gets left out," Christopher said, unbothered. "What about this drum? He can get in touch with his inner Inuit."

"Nah, we should get him this." She held up a totem pole with staring eyes and a green mask over flaring red nostrils. "It kind of looks like him."

Christopher grinned. "You're right."

Lainie picked it up and carried it to the cashier to sign for it. "Gift wrapped and delivered to my room," she said when she returned. "You gotta love it."

Christopher exhaled and flexed his shoulders. "Okay, are we done with shopping now?"

"Listen to you. We stopped at one store. I swear, guys are such wusses about shopping."

"We're not wusses," he corrected as they walked out. "We just think there are better ways to use our time."

"Oh, yeah, like watching ESPN and ESPN2 and ESPN Classic and ESPN University and...have I missed any?"

"Fox Sports, New England Sports Network, the NFL Network, the Golf Channel, the Hockey Channel, the Yankee Channel," he ticked off, shaking his head in disappointment. "Get with the program, Lainie. You had three brothers running around the house, for cripe's sake."

"I know. It's a wonder I wasn't more deeply scarred by the experience. Oh, wait—" She broke off as they passed a shop with photo-lined walls. "We have to pick up that picture we took yesterday for Mom and Dad."

The hundreds of toothy grins that surrounded them as they walked into the store were vaguely oppressive. The walls, the ranks of freestanding shelves, seemingly every flat surface was covered with row after row of photos: pictures of passengers at karaoke, passengers at dinner, passengers cooking in the Culinary Arts Center, passengers standing with the tableau of stuffed penguins. The cruise line was remarkably effective at coming up with ways of separating passengers from their money, Christopher reflected.

Lainie wandered down the rows looking at the dates posted at the top. "Aha," she pounced. "Captain's reception. Oh, look, here's the picture of all of us."

It showed the group of them crowded together, grinning into the camera. It seemed natural to see Larkin and her father there.

"Hey, here's the shot of Speed and I," Lainie said, pulling it loose to admire it. "Doesn't he look cute?"

"You're probably a better judge of that than I am."

"Grab the ones of Jacob's and Gabe's families," she directed, still enjoying the picture of her husband.

Even as Christopher reached for the other photographs, he saw the one of Larkin and him together.

They weren't staring into the camera like the people in all the other photos. Instead, they looked at each other,

Larkin's mouth curving into that brilliant smile of hers, her eyes gleaming with mischief.

And for a fleeting moment, it felt so right.

"You like her, huh?"

He glanced up to find Lainie studying him. "Yeah."

"Nice to see that for a change. I was worried that your hormones had gone out of whack."

"Not out of whack, just out of batteries. There's something about working eighteen hours a day that'll do that to you."

"I'm glad you were able to take a break and come along. I mean, I'm sorry Nick and Sloane couldn't make it, but it's been nice to spend a little time with you again."

"Yeah, it's been too long."

They walked up front with the pictures and signed for them. "So is something going to happen with you and Larkin?" she asked as they headed back out to the gallery.

"You're subtle."

Lainie grinned. "I pride myself on it. So?"

"What exactly are you expecting? There's tonight, that's it. Tomorrow, we dock in Vancouver."

"Yeah. Too bad there aren't things like telephones and e-mail and airplanes."

The humor faded. "You don't give up, do you?"

"That's because you're not really answering the question."

He moved his shoulders. "Lainie, she's a trust-fund baby. She shows up in magazines. She probably lives in Beverly Hills. I'm a half broke—mostly broke—farmer who lives in the sticks. You want to tell me how you can see that working any better than it did before?"

"How do you know she doesn't want something different?"

He shook his head. "I'd like to think that I learned enough from the fiasco with Nicole not to make the same mistake twice."

Lainie shook her head. "Christopher, they're not even remotely the same. Every sentence Nicole ever spoke started with the word *I*. Larkin's not like that. Where is she right now? Hitting golf balls with her dad, and I can guarantee it's not for her entertainment."

"What do you want me to say?" he snapped. "We're going to live happily ever after? Give it up, Lainie. It's not going to happen. We'll have a good time tonight, and then we'll call it quits. End of story."

She studied the picture and then pressed it into his hand. "All I've got to say is take a look at this, champ. If you ask me, it doesn't look like end of story. It looks like the beginning."

"Fore!" Larkin called.

Carter's lips twitched. "Are you warning salmon on the fairway?"

"You never know," she said with dignity, then ruined it by cursing a blue streak when her ball slanted to the right.

"Still got that slice, I see."

They stood on a little patch of artificial turf on the top deck of the ship, driving balls out over the water.

"Dad, the only person I play golf with is you."

"Hmmph." He stepped up, addressed the ball and went into his backswing. "Doesn't have to be that way. You're a strong girl. You could be a good player if you tried."

"If I ever decide to become a doctor, I'll keep it in mind." There was a loud thwack as his driver connected to the ball. Larkin watched it go sailing out over the water. "Goodbye, little Titleist. You sleep with the fishes tonight."

"Are you ever going to go back and finish college?" Carter asked as she stepped onto the turf.

"Not unless there's something I want to do that requires it. I don't see the point."

"You don't feel the need for a career?"

"I model, remember?"

"That's not a real job."

Larkin drew her club back and slammed the ball as hard as she could. "Tell that to Giselle Bündchen."

"I mean for you. You can do more than go to parties and stand around looking pretty."

She met his eyes. "Correct me if I'm wrong but I seem to recall that the last time we had this conversation, we didn't speak for five years," she said levelly. "Are you really sure you want to keep going with this?"

Carter stared at her and then, to her everlasting shock, threw back his head and guffawed. "Oh, Larkin, you're a credit to your old man. It's too bad you never went into business. You'd have mowed them down."

"I'm not sure I want to mow them down," she said, unmollified.

"Oh, you will, one of these days. I don't know when and I don't know how, but you will." He slung an arm around her neck. "Come on. What do you say we go inside and you buy your old man a drink?"

Christopher took a deep breath and knocked on Molly's stateroom door.

It opened up almost immediately. "Hey, no fair showing— Oh, Christopher. Hi. Come in." Surprised pleasure filled her voice. "I thought you were Carter."

"Carter?"

"He's coming by to pick me up for dinner. What did you need?"

"I was hoping to talk with you for a couple minutes."

"Of course, come in. Just don't mind me if I keep getting ready." She picked up her jewelry box. "A woman's entitled to some vanity."

"You have a thing for him."

She glanced over from putting on her earrings. "I enjoy his company, if that's what you mean."

Christopher took his time going to a chair, searching for the right words. "I'm not trying to pry, Aunt Molly, but how much do you know about him?"

"Carter? What he's told me, why?" She set the earring down. "What's this all about, Christopher?"

He hesitated. "We're a little concerned," he said finally. "You've been spending a lot of time with him. We just…"

"Christopher, we're on a weeklong cruise. I don't expect a full biography. I don't really expect anything."

He met her gaze. "Part of my job when I was in Washington was to follow the financial industry."

"Did you know Carter?"

"Only by reputation. Are you aware that he's been divorced?"

"Yes. Four times, as a matter of fact." She laughed at his expression. "Christopher, the man's sixty. He's got a past. We all do." Her gaze softened. "It's sweet of you boys to worry about me. And I assume when you say 'we,' you mean Jacob, don't you?"

"Well…"

"I appreciate the thought. But honestly, I'm not expecting anything from Carter, except maybe an escort to dinner tonight. He's the city mouse, I'm the country mouse. He's got millions of dollars, I'm thrilled that I won five hundred dollars in bingo." She adjusted her necklace and rose. "Different worlds, and that's okay. I've had a better time this week than I've had in years. Part of that's due to all of you, but part of it's due to him, too. It's been a lovely surprise to step out of my life for a week and have some excitement. And tomorrow, I'll be ready to get back home."

Christopher leaned back and let out a long breath.

Molly regarded him with amusement. "That worried over this conversation?"

"Aunt Molly, you have no idea," he said feelingly.

"Well, I'm glad you stepped in. This would have been sheer torture for Jacob."

He nodded. "That's why I offered. And because I was concerned, too."

"Well, now you can relax. You've done your job and all is well." She gave him a speculative glance. "Turnabout is fair play, though. You and Larkin seem pretty interested in one another. What's going on there?"

He shrugged. "You just did a better job of answering the question than I ever could. She's the daughter of someone who's got millions, she lives in L.A., she's a model. I think that pretty much covers it all."

Molly walked over and kissed him on the cheek. "There's still time to have a lovely evening tonight. And if there's one thing I've learned after sixty-four years on this planet, it's that you never really know what will happen."

There was a knock on the door. Anticipation lit her face, and suddenly he knew what she'd looked like as a girl. "Excuse me, I think that's my dinner date."

Chandeliers, crystal, candlelight. A procession of flaming Baked Alaskas. The Trasks sat around the table at dinner, Carter next to Molly, Larkin next to Christopher, the rest of the group spreading out in all directions. Strange to think the week before, she and Carter had stared across the room enviously at this family. Now, for this one night, they were honorary members.

Gabe clinked the edge of his knife against his water glass to tame the laughter. "Hey, guys, quiet down. Mom wants to say something."

"Well." Molly shifted Keegan to one side on her lap and cleared her throat. "I just wanted to thank you all. It's just been such a delight, getting to spend time with you, seeing the glaciers, all of it. I know you had to take time off work to come here, and I want you to know how much it means to me that we did this together. I feel so lucky to have a family like you." She gave a warm glance to Carter and Larkin. "And to have new friends to count, too. I really am blessed. To all of you." She raised her glass.

"Right back at you," Gabe said.

Around the table, there was the clink of goblet to goblet.

Christopher drank, then raised his glass again. "While we're at it, I'd just like to propose a toast to Aunt Molly's world-famous chocolate double-nut brownies. I know that I wouldn't be where I am in my life today if I hadn't had a regular supply growing up." He turned to Molly. "Although I am running a little low, in case you're bored in the next few days after we get home."

The murmurs of agreement changed to catcalls with his final words.

"While we're in the middle of this group hug," Gabe said, "on behalf of parents, I'd just like to thank the baby-sitting contingent for their efforts. Mom, Christopher, Lainie, J.J., you've made everybody's trip a little bit better." He started to drink and stopped. "And if you're, you know, bored and at loose ends tonight, I've got a job for you. After all, I'm good for paying it back if you ever need it."

"Good thing. You're about to get your chance," Lainie told him.

"What, are you guys getting a dog?"

"No." She looked around the table, eyes gleaming with excitement. "We're pregnant."

"Oh, Lainie!" Molly set Keegan on the ground and threw her arms around Lainie. "I'm so happy for you."

"I knew it," Celic crowed. "I was telling Jacob when we were getting dressed, nobody could talk about chocolate-covered Doritos without being pregnant."

"Although it does have potential as a snack food," Lainie argued.

"Yeah. Have that baby and get back to me on that," Celie said.

J.J. coughed. "Babies."

"What?"

"The doctor thinks he's detected two heartbeats," Lainie said, nodding at Sophia and Adam. "I guess twins run in the family."

Gabe shook his head. "You're in for it now, dude."

"Get used to not sleeping," Jacob advised.

"It's not that bad," Celie scolded.

"You had pregnancy hormones to help you. *Hey.*" He rubbed his arm where she'd punched it, giving her a re-proachful look. "I didn't say it wasn't worth it. Most of the time," he qualified, watching Gerard push a straw up his nose.

"Well, I'm thrilled to hear your news." Molly kissed J.J.'s cheek and sat back down. "Do your parents know?"

"We called them before dinner. We would have said something to everyone sooner but we wanted to make sure we made it into the third month all clear."

"And have you?" Molly asked.

J.J. smiled broadly. "She's gotten straight A's on every report card."

Carter signaled the waiter. "Clicquot all around," he said, "and one sparkling cider. We've got a lot more toasts to make."

"Here's to that," Lainie said.

J.J. kissed her hair. "Here's to you."

* * *

The wood of the deck was washed to a silvery glow as Carter escorted Molly out onto the fantail. The wake of the ship formed a white effervescence in the moonlight.

"It's enough to make you believe in magic, isn't it?" Molly asked. "Like if you looked hard enough you'd see a mermaid splashing out there in the waves."

"Do you believe in mermaids?"

"I'd believe in anything after this week." She sighed. "It's been like a dream."

"I'm glad we got to spend time together. You've given me a lot to think about."

"You're giving me too much credit. I think you've been mulling over all of those things already. You just weren't aware of it."

"You made me aware of it."

She moved her shoulders. "Carter, there's nothing particularly noble or special about what I do. I just live and do the best I can."

"And you don't understand what I find to admire?"

"If you don't like what you're doing, change it," she said simply. "You can afford to do whatever you want. Just…"

"Just what?"

"Don't put it off. Life's uncertain, you and I know that more than most. So if you want to change your life, do it. You should be happy, too."

"I am," he said quietly.

She blushed. "It's been a wonderful week, simply lovely." She sighed.

"It has been." He smiled. "Especially getting to know you."

Molly looked up at him. For a moment they stood in the moonlight, the silver washing the years away. Her hand reached out to catch his. He pulled her closer. And as the waves parted around them, he leaned down and they kissed.

"I've got to hand it to your family," Larkin told Christopher. "It's never dull."

His teeth gleamed. "Kind of hard to be when there are as many of us as there are."

They sat in the cocktail lounge attached to the top deck of the ship. Windows encircled the darkened room, putting the focus on the moonlit water and the narrows all around them.

A martini sat on the table before her. She already felt a little giddy. He'd seemed distant the previous night but now he was back. "I like your family. They're so nice."

"That's because they like you." Christopher raised her hand to his lips. "And so do I."

Her pulse rate sped up. The shadows threw his features into relief. "Let's dance," she said impulsively.

"All right." He led her onto the floor, spinning her up against him, then leaning her back for a dip.

Larkin laughed and whirled around and when the music stopped, sank back down in her chair. "Who knew I'd go off on a cruise and end up with a cattleman?"

"Not exactly cattleman."

"All right, a dairy farmer. A milkman."

"Chèvre."

"What?"

"I make chèvre."

Her eyes widened. "As in goat cheese?"

"Yeah."

"You have a herd of goats?" Her lips twitched.

"A hundred head."

"Oh, my God, you've got to be kidding." A giggle escaped before she clapped her hand over her mouth.

"Glad I can amuse you," he said, but his voice didn't sound amused at all.

"I'm sorry, it's just…you, as a goatherd."

He stiffened. "A goatherd meets a model on a cruise," he said flatly. "It kind of sounds like the setup for a bad joke."

"That wasn't what I meant," she said. "It's just that when you said dairy farmer, I thought you meant cows. You know, milk and cream? I didn't think of you—" a snort of laughter escaped "—leading around a herd of nanny goats." And at that image, the laughter just took over until she was lying back helplessly, tears streaming from her eyes, attracting stares from the people around them.

"I want her drink," someone said.

Every time she tried to stop, the laughter would break out again. Finally she got control of it. "I'm sorry," she said, wiping her eyes. "It wasn't even what you said. I just…you know how you just get laughing sometimes."

"Yeah, sure," he said.

"Christopher, don't get angry. I wasn't laughing at you."

"Of course you weren't. Look, compared to what you're used to, it isn't the most glamorous occupation, I get that. They don't do spreads on us for *Vanity Fair.* But it's an honest job, and it means something to me. Someone who really worked for a living could appreciate that."

The giddiness evaporated. "That wasn't necessary."

He blew out a breath. "No, you're right. It probably wasn't." He shook his head, tossed a bill on the table and rose. "Look, it's late. We're both tired, and if we keep going, we're going to wreck the whole week. So why don't we just say good-night and forget the past five minutes ever happened?"

The problem was, she thought as he walked out, they had.

* * *

What kind of sick person decided to have a ship dock at seven in the morning? Larkin wondered as she stumbled half awake down the gangway. After a peaceful, idyllic week of making their own schedules, suddenly everything was hustle and bustle. The sun was barely above the horizon and they were lining up to clear customs, filling out forms, hunting down their luggage amid rows of hundreds of other bags. The return to the real world was all too abrupt. She wasn't ready for it.

She didn't want to look at Christopher. How could things have gone from good to bad so quickly, and why hadn't he given her the benefit of the doubt? Instead, he'd shut her out and shut her down.

Behind Larkin, Carter handed Molly a business card. "My cell phone number is on here. I hope you'll use it."

Molly studied the heavy, embossed card and glanced up at him. "I can't say I have a business card to give you in return, but we do have a Web site. If you're ever up our way, please stop in."

"You can depend on it. Do you need me to get you a cab?"

"Oh, no. We've got a van coming." She waved back over at the rest of the family. "I've got plenty of menfolk to take care of me."

"As long as you're taken care of."

"I am, thank you."

"I think you're still missing something, though." Carter reached in his pocket and pulled out a small box. "Happy homecoming."

She frowned. "Carter, what have you done? That's not fair, coming up with a surprise present."

"I'd like to say it's a piece of gold-sprayed macaroni art I made just for you, but my talents don't run in that direction. Just take it and say thank you."

"Thank you." Molly shook her head. "It had better not be something expensive, that's all I have to say."

"Open it and find out."

Flicking him a glance, she opened the box and unwrapped the tissue paper–covered object inside. Then stared. "But…but how did you…" It was the crystal polar bear she'd admired in Juneau.

"You liked it."

"Yes, but we got back to the boat half an hour before we sailed."

He grinned. "I ran track in college. Amazing how fast you can move when you're worried you're going to see the ship pulling away on you."

"Carter, I can't take this."

"Sure you can. You liked it and I wanted to get you something to remember the cruise by." And him, though he didn't say it. "Consider it a Valentine's Day present."

It made her smile, as he'd intended. "Valentine's Day is five months away, you loon."

"I love it when you sweet-talk me."

A taxi whipped around the curve that led in from the street and screeched to a stop before them. At Carter's nod, the stevedores loaded their luggage and opened the door for Larkin.

She turned to Molly. "It was nice to meet you," she said and gave her a brief hug. It would be simple, she thought. She'd already said goodbye to the other Trasks. All she had to do was get in the cab and drive away without a backward glance. There was no need to say anything to Christopher at all.

But she couldn't help looking over at him.

He stood, watching her. When he saw her turn, he gave a little half-assed wave.

It was better this way, Larkin told herself, gritting her

teeth as she got into the cab. What would've happened if they'd slept together the night before? Maybe the big goodbye kiss, trading addresses and phone numbers? And what good would it have done? Christopher was right, they had different lives, different expectations. Exchanging contact information would just have made it all the harder because if she knew anything, she knew damned good and well relationships didn't last. There was no point in fooling themselves. The minute they drove away from the pier, the memories would start to fade. They'd get home, lose those slips of paper and soon the only thing that would remind them of the trip would be the photograph they'd taken.

And one day, they'd lose that, too.

Better to have it end this way. No false hopes, no false promises. End of story.

There was a knock on the window. She glanced up to see Christopher. Adrenaline vaulted through her. For a moment, she just stared, then she rolled down the window.

"Almost forgot," he said. "I've got a goodbye present for you." And he handed her the charger for her Black-Berry. "Fly safe," he said and turned away.

"Airport, please," Carter said.

"Departures," Larkin snapped.

Chapter Eight

"At least he gave your charger back," Reyna said as she held a black Prada skirt to her waist and eyed herself critically in the mirror.

Larkin glared at her former roommate. "The man knocked on the window and gave it to me as a goodbye present. And then he told me to fly safe," she snapped.

"Well, he could've kept it," Reyna pointed out. "Then you'd not only be ticked off but you'd have to buy a new one. I mean, really, what's more important, your Black-Berry or some joker you met on a cruise? It's not like you were expecting true love, were you?"

"Of course not." Larkin crossed to a rack of jeans.

The last thing she was thinking about was anything long-term with Christopher Trask. Or with anybody, for that matter. She shook her head impatiently. It was just that it had wrecked everything. They'd been having a good time and then he'd gotten all prickly. Granted, she probably shouldn't have laughed but then he hadn't needed to make that crack about working for a living.

They could have danced themselves into exhaustion. They could have—good Lord—they could have had head-board-banging sex. They could have....

They could have had fun. But instead, things had to get all crunchy. One minute, everything was great. The next, it had all gone wrong.

Such a stupid little argument. Then again, why was she surprised? That was what relationships were made of. That had always been the way with Carter and his wives, one stupid argument after another, salted with lies, until the arguments became pitched battles and the battles eventually became the end. The moral of her story was that relationships just weren't worth it.

Not that she would dignify a few days of flirtation on a cruise with the term *relationship*. No matter how good the kisses had been.

But the worst part, the part that completely fried her, was that she missed him. For all that she was still annoyed at him, she just missed having him to talk to, to laugh with. She missed that feeling of connection. And she hated the fact that she would always wonder how it would have been with him, what would've happened.

What had happened was nothing, end of story. Christopher Trask didn't signify. He was just another face in a photograph to stick in a drawer somewhere, another memory to bring out on a long, sleepless night.

Too bad she was having so much trouble sleeping these days.

"Your total comes to $38.70," Molly Trask said to the stout blonde on the other side of the counter, sliding the credit card slip across to her. "If I could just have your signature, please?"

The wide-planked maple floors of the Trask Farm gift shop gleamed with polish, red gingham curtains hanging at the windows. On the pine shelves, oven mitts and dish towels jostled for position with mugs and teapots, puzzles and plush toys, lemon curd and jellies. And, of course, maple everything, from syrup to candy to maple pepper and ice cream. Something for everybody was Molly's philosophy, and if there was one word she most wanted to evoke, it was *welcoming*.

"I can't wait to give my sister the pot holder," the woman said. "She collects frogs. She'll love it."

"Where are you from?" Molly asked.

"Minnetonka, Minnesota."

"I've heard that's beautiful country."

"Dick, that's my husband—" she nodded at a stocky man in a purple Vikings ball cap "—he says he wouldn't live anywhere else. Although if we ever got rich, I'd buy a place here and run a gift shop just like this in the summer and fall. You're so lucky."

"That's what I tell myself every day," Molly said lightly. "Thank you so much, Mrs. Sorenson."

"Oh, just Peggy," she said.

"Peggy," Molly repeated. "It was a pleasure to meet you. Enjoy the leaves and travel safely back to Minnesota." She watched them walk to the little hall that led to the front door.

Lucky, she mused, looking around the shop. It was how she'd always felt. Even after she'd been widowed, life had been so full. She had family, she had friends in the tight-knit Eastmont community she'd lived in for over forty years. Any yen she might have had for new experiences was usually satisfied by the people she met at the shop, or her yearly trip to the big craft and gift shop conference. She'd thought herself happy and content.

And now, suddenly, she wasn't.

Molly made an impatient noise and began dusting shelves. She was just being silly. Foolish to get her head turned by a week spent living in the lap of luxury, being waited on hand and foot like some exotic princess. Manicures and massages, fancy gowns and food. Laughing every night over five-course dinners.

And basking in the attentions of an interesting, attractive man.

She'd known it was just a shipboard adventure. It didn't matter. She still felt a bit like the sun had been switched off. It would take more than a week for her to stop comparing one life to the other, she supposed. It would take more than a week to stop remembering that kiss in the moonlight.

"Look at you, Molly Trask," she muttered under her breath, "mooning like you're some teenager." Annoyed at herself, she picked up a moose cookie jar with ceramic horns and began dusting it off as the front door jingled. Clean stock and new customers were her life. Alaska had been lovely, but it was over. She'd always been happy with what she had. She would be again, once the glamour wore off.

She just needed to get back in the swing of things.

"Got any sugar I can borrow?"

She jumped and turned to see Carter Hayes. The cookie jar dropped from her suddenly nerveless fingers to shatter on the floor.

"Oh!"

"Ah, hell," he said, stepping forward. "I'm sorry, Molly. I shouldn't have startled you." He crouched and began tossing shards into what was left of the jar. "Let me clean this up. And pay for it, of course."

"It was an ugly old thing anyway." She crouched down

beside him, shaking her head. "We've had it for years. I can't imagine what possessed me to think anyone was ever going to buy it."

"You never know," he said. "Just because something's been waiting around for a few years doesn't mean that it isn't exactly what somebody wants." He leaned in to kiss her cheek. "It's nice to see you."

"What are you doing here?"

"At the moment, picking up broken pottery. Can you get me a dustpan?"

She went behind the counter and brought one back. "Outside of cleaning the floor, what are you doing here? Not that it's not nice to see you, too."

"Oh, I was in the neighborhood and thought I'd drop by."

"Montclair?"

"Manhattan."

She put a hand on her hip. "You are aware that New York is five hours away, right?"

He grinned. "'Zat so? Maybe I just wanted to see you, then." He pulled a little mum blossom out of his shirt pocket and handed it to her.

"What's that for?"

"Valentine's Day," he said.

"Valentine's Day still isn't for months."

"Oh, my mistake." He rose with a dustpan full of pottery shards. "So tell me where the trash can is, and then you can show me around this place of yours."

Christopher ran the gas-powered grass trimmer beneath the pasture fence, cutting away the undergrowth that was encroaching on the bottom strand of the electrified wire. There was something to be said for a job that kept a guy going from dawn to well after dark. Especially after a week off, it left him exhausted and likely to tumble into a dead sleep at night.

Too bad it didn't keep him too exhausted to think during the day.

Larkin. It made no damned sense to still have her on his mind. She was probably back living her life, clubbing, walking down runways or whatever the hell it was she did. Different worlds, he reminded himself. There was no point in dwelling on it.

No point in missing her.

Christopher heard a horn honk and saw a truck he recognized as his aunt's roll up the drive to the farm. Switching off his trimmer and pulling off his work gloves, he made his way down to meet her.

She stepped out of the truck laughing. Next to her, he saw, was Carter Hayes. And they were holding hands.

Christopher's eyes narrowed.

"Look who showed up," Molly said.

"I see that. So what are you doing out in the sticks?" he asked as he walked up to them. As if he couldn't see the reason plain before him.

"Good to see you, too, Christopher," Carter replied mildly.

"Sorry, hanging out with goats kind of wrecks your manners." He dredged up a polite smile and wiped off his hands before extending one to Carter. "Good to see you again. How are you?"

"Fine." Carter shook. "So's Larkin, in case you were wondering."

Christopher did his best to ignore the flash of regret. "Glad to hear it."

"I stopped in to see Molly. She gave me some of your cheese for lunch. I wanted to come by and see where you make it." He scanned the grounds. "The place looks good."

"You wouldn't believe how much work he's put into it," Molly said.

Christopher shrugged. "Here and there. I still haven't quite decided whether I'm making an investment or indulging in an expensive hobby, but we're making progress. You want a tour?"

Carter nodded. "That would be great."

It was interesting, Christopher discovered, to see the farm through someone else's eyes. All too often, his days were an accumulation of one task after another, in between supervising Deke, his hired hand, or whatever intern he had at the time. When he looked around the pine-shingled outbuildings, the hilly pastures, the animal pens, all he saw was the jobs he needed to get to, the improvements waiting to happen. Rare were the days he could get to those improvements. Rarer still were the days he could come out in the morning, take a deep breath and consciously appreciate living his dream. The wow factor, as he'd told Larkin, fell by the wayside. Seeing it through Carter's eyes reminded him of all he valued about his life.

And all that he stood to lose.

"So you've got a dairy as well as chickens, hogs and cattle," Carter ticked off as they walked out of the barn. "Is that usual?"

"I'm not sure there is such a thing as usual for a small farmer. I raise the chickens and hogs to bring in some extra money from meat sales. The cattle I just do for myself and the rest of the family." He latched the door behind them. "And because I don't have enough of a challenge already."

"It looks like it's enough to keep you busy."

"More than." Christopher let them out of the holding pen that surrounded the barn, and into the drive. They'd come full circle, just as it appeared Christopher had, with the end of his life there almost in sight. He consciously warded off the thought. "My ex-colleagues in the financial community might question the return on investment, but it has its perks."

"You used to work in Washington, right?" Carter asked.

He nodded. "And Manhattan. For the financial industry."

"Why the change?"

"Everything gets old. I wanted something where I could take a look at the end of the day and see something concrete I'd done, something I'd made."

Carter shot him a sharp glance. "I can understand that." His gaze swept the property, both taking in the scenery before him and somehow miles away at the same time. "Just walk away from it all," he murmured. "Wake up every morning to a place like this." And abruptly, as though something had clicked inside him, he looked at Molly and Christopher. "That's what I need, this kind of place. This kind of work."

Christopher chuckled. "I'm sure you could find someone to sell you one. But I wouldn't recommend it."

Carter looked at him. "Why not? You don't think I could run a place like this?"

"I don't think you'd want to, once you tried it. And it's not the sort of thing you can do halfway. If you're looking for a country place, you can find plenty of houses around here on an acre or two. Grab one, plant some tomatoes, enjoy the fresh air."

Carter shook his head. "I said I want a change. I didn't say I wanted to stop working. I'm not the type of guy to just sit on his butt all day. A farm like this would give me something to dig into."

Where to start, Christopher wondered wearily. "Carter, with all due respect, I don't think you understand what you'd be getting into."

"No way to find out but to do it."

His first impulse was to leave Carter to step in it on his own, but then Christopher glanced over at Molly. She watched Carter, her expression a mixture of curiosity, anxiety and, yes, affection. However misguided Carter's current idea might be, he was important to her. Christopher shoved his hands in his back pockets and looked around the barnyard, then back at Carter. "All right. If you really want to do this, then I'll teach you."

"What?"

"Hold off on buying a place at first. Intern for me," he suggested. "I'll show you what I know." He stopped. "At least for as long as I can."

"Meaning?"

"Sometimes you farm to pay the bills, and sometimes you pay the bills to farm. I'm probably going to have to put the place up on the block before the year is out."

Molly stared at him. "Christopher, what are you talking about?"

"Like I said, it's not working out. Or at least it's not working out well enough fast enough. The money's pretty much gone, Aunt Molly. There's not much else I can do besides sell. You can intern until I do, Carter. After that, you're on your own. Shoot, you'll probably be able to get this place cheap," he added with a grin that didn't quite make it.

Molly reached out and squeezed his hand. "I'm so sorry."

He moved his shoulders, warding off the sympathy. "It's okay. I gave it a good go. I'll head back to Washington, and who knows, maybe come back and try again once I've made some money."

"That's one possibility." Carter studied him. "I can think of another."

Chapter Nine

He was out of his mind, Larkin thought as she stomped on the accelerator of the rental Audi and swung through the curves of the twisty Vermont road. Carter had to be out of his mind. A man didn't just toss aside forty years as a futures trader to become a…a goat farmer. To play golf and live in the islands, maybe. To dig manure? Hardly.

Of course, he wasn't really nuts. What he was was in the hands of a sharpster who'd turned happenstance into opportunity.

Christopher Trask. Just the thought of him made her blood boil. He'd had the gall to act offended on the cruise when she'd accused him of trying to get next to Carter. *Carter has nothing to do with this,* he'd said. Her hands tightened on the wheel as she remembered the feel of his mouth crushed to hers. He'd offered it as proof, and like a sap, she'd believed it. Now, the minute her back was turned, here he was trying to dip his hand into Carter's wallet.

Over her dead body.

On the side of the road, a sign said "Doe Si Doe Farm, 100 feet ahead."

You ever wind up in Vermont, stop in and see me.

"Stop in and see me, my ass," Larkin muttered.

"Left turn, twenty feet," said the calm voice of the GPS unit.

"Shut up." Larkin flipped on her blinker and swung up a tree-lined road, the pavement dappled with morning sun.

Oh, she was going to stop in and see Christopher Trask, all right. And blow his little con job right out of the water. She wasn't about to stand by and watch her father gallop into yet another marital fiasco, especially not one that came with half ownership in a goat farm.

A goat farm, for God's sake.

The pavement turned to hard-packed dirt, the car jouncing over the ruts. Oh, sure, she could see Carter in his suits tooling around out here. What had Christopher used, hypnosis? Or just Molly Trask?

Larkin stomped on the brake and brought the Audi to a sliding stop. An ornate wooden sign hung by a narrow gravel drive that wound up between two granite posts. Almost straight up. She backed and turned into the drive, cresting a rise to enter a packed-dirt parking area.

And a whole different world.

She'd never been on a farm before, but if she'd been asked to imagine one, it would have been like this. To one side rose a white, two-story farmhouse with green shutters and a broad veranda running along the front. Next to it stood an old-fashioned barn, its wood-shingled sides weathered to a soft grayish-brown, red-trimmed windows letting in the light along the raised central spine of the roof. Other outbuildings in the same tidy buff and red color scheme encircled the parking area. Next to them, the grassy, fenced-in pastures looked almost unnaturally green. The overall effect was neat, pastoral and charming.

Assuming you were in a mood to be charmed.

Larkin got out and slammed the door, her kitten-heeled pumps wobbling a bit in the gravel. Behind her, she heard what sounded like the playground yelp of a fourth grader, then another. Frowning, she looked over to the little fenced-in grassy meadow next to a smaller barn that sat across from the first. In a nearby pen, white chickens scratched in the dust. A tall, lanky man who looked like an extra from the set of *Deliverance* filled a bucket from a tap.

Wrinkling her nose at the smell as she passed the chicken pen, Larkin marched up to him. "Christopher Trask."

He squinted up at her and straightened. "Uh, no, I'm Deke, not Christopher."

"I know," she said, exasperated. "Where is he?"

Deke took off his ball cap, adjusted the brim nervously and put it back on. "Well, he just got done milking, so I think he's… That is to say, I guess he's…"

"Here," said a familiar voice.

Larkin turned furiously and her jaw dropped. It was Christopher but not as she'd ever seen him before. He wore a beat-up Red Sox hat, a pair of worn and faded jeans, a sleeveless sweatshirt and the kind of heavy leather work boots that could give a girl ideas.

It didn't matter, suddenly, that she'd always gone for stylish, sophisticated men. It didn't matter that the country look wasn't her thing. All she could do was stare as Christopher crossed the yard carrying some sort of big metal canister, muscles shifting in his arms as he walked. He looked strong, capable, immensely confident.

And outrageously sexy.

Enough, she told herself as he came to a stop before her. No drooling allowed. It interfered with strangling.

Christopher set the canister down and rested his hands on his hips. It was a milk can, she saw, of the sort usually used for restaurant decorations where she came from.

Not here, apparently.

He surveyed her. "The Governator?" He nodded at the novelty Arnold Schwarzenegger T-shirt she wore. She flushed.

She'd been having cocktails with a girlfriend when she'd gotten Carter's call. "I'm moving to Vermont," he'd said. "Your old man's going to be a farmer." She'd been out the door and on her way to LAX before they'd even hung up. She still wore the miniskirt she'd had on; the T-shirt had been a last-minute airport buy, along with a toothbrush.

"I took a red-eye out," she said.

His eyebrows rose a fraction. "When I said drop in anytime, I had no idea you'd be in such a hurry."

"Really?" she asked sweetly. "I'm a little surprised you weren't expecting it, considering you conned my father into sinking a small fortune into this fiasco of yours."

What she'd expected, she couldn't say, but certainly not for him to laugh.

"Stop it," she snapped.

"I can't think of anyone less likely to be conned than your father," he said.

"You think a man like Carter Hayes belongs on a farm mucking out goat pens?"

"I think a man like Carter Hayes belongs wherever he feels like being. Anyway, what do you care? Pissed off that it's eating into your inheritance?"

"I'm pissed off because you lied."

"What do you mean, I lied?"

"You told me you wouldn't take money from him."

"I don't believe the subject of money ever came up."

"Yes, it did," she said furiously. "You gave me your word. You said—"

He took a swift step and pulled her against him. Larkin pressed her hands against his chest, but it was like pressing against the side of the barn. She smelled grass, a hint of the soap he'd used that morning and the clean scent of the outdoors. He leaned closer, and her muscles began to weaken.

"What I said was that what was between you and me had nothing to do with Carter," he said softly. "And that's still true."

Just as her lips were beginning to shudder apart, he released her and strode away toward the smaller barn. It took her only a moment to recover and chase after him.

"Where's my father?" she demanded. "I want to talk to him."

"He's in Manhattan." The words were curt. "He left yesterday to go wind up some business. He should be back in a week or so."

"Sure. Back to bail you out."

For an instant, a muscle jumped in his jaw, but he mastered his annoyance. "Look, whatever you think of this, it wasn't my idea."

She snorted.

Christopher pulled open the door to the barn. Inside, a pen held a collection of small pigs, both black with white splotches and pink. They crowded around the feed trough as Christopher upended the metal canister to dump in a load of something unidentifiable that Larkin supposed functioned as food.

She followed him inside. "So you're trying to tell me he just out of the blue decided to throw his whole life away and come here?"

"Apparently it's his idea of retirement."

"Mucking out goat pens?"

Christopher headed through the barn to the back door. "Yep—although the way he figures it, he's not throwing his life away."

"And if the way he figures it means more money for your farm, so much the better."

Christopher swung around to face her. "Like I said, it wasn't my idea. But to his credit, he seems serious about making some changes in his life. Why begrudge him the opportunity to try it out—or work it out of his system?"

"I don't begrudge him, I begrudge you," she shot back.

"But it's not about me. It's about your dad. He wants to try his hand at working outside for a change, get away from the office fluorescents before he starts looking like a cave fish. Believe me, I know where he's coming from. You would, too, if you'd worked like he has."

"Oh, what, if I were more evolved I'd be mucking out the goat pens right next to him?"

"You'd have to be much more evolved." He gave her a mocking look. "Your father might actually stick with it for a while. You wouldn't last a week."

"What's that supposed to mean?"

Ignoring her, he stepped outside into the little fenced-in pasture.

Larkin took two quick steps after him. "I'm still talking to—" She yelped and lurched against him as her heel broke.

Christopher caught her to him. For a whirling instant, their lips almost touched. Then he leaned his head away and stood her up. "Well, as you can see, it's kind of hard on the Jimmy Choos. Face it. You're not made for hard work. You're made to read your trust-fund statements, talk on your BlackBerry and pout for the camera." He looked her up and down. "Your dad wants something else in his life besides shuffling money around. For my own reasons, I've decided to help him find out if this is what he's looking for."

"Out of the goodness of your heart?"

"Does it matter? Look, you can throw as big a temper tantrum as you want, but I think you know your father better than I do, and even I know he's going to do this until he decides he wants to do something else. So you may as well go back to the mansion or the boat or wherever the hell it is you hang out and deal with it." He turned to walk away.

"I'll deal with it all right." She took a few uneven steps and stopped to yank her shoes off. "I'll deal with it right here."

"Excuse me?" He turned back.

Larkin drew herself up. "I'm not leaving until he gets back."

"This isn't a hotel. It's a working farm," he said scornfully. "I don't have the time or resources to put up anybody who isn't pulling their weight."

The flash of temper in Larkin's eyes could have burnt toast. "What makes you think I couldn't pull my weight?"

"Oh, please." He walked past her to the metal gate that led back to the barnyard.

She followed him, grabbing the wire of the fence.

And yelped as she snatched her hand back from the quick jolt that ran through her. "It's electrified," she accused.

"Of course it is. You're on a farm. The fences are designed to keep the animals in." He slanted her a look. "And predators out."

All the anger coalesced. "I'm sick of everybody telling me what I can and can't do," she said hotly. "I could keep up with anybody on this farm if I wanted to."

He gave a short laugh. "That I'd like to see."

"Fine." She marched up to him until her chin was practically on his chest. "Fine. You think I couldn't last a week? I'll stay two."

"Two weeks?" The bored, amused tone only infuriated her further. "I bet you'd be bitching to the high heavens after an hour and ready to bolt after two."

"You want to make a bet?" she demanded. "Two weeks. I work for you doing anything you want."

"Right." His tone was mocking.

"And if I make it through the two weeks," she continued, eyes gleaming, "you turn down Carter's money."

He snorted. "Why would I do that? If I needed money bad enough to accept your father's offer, I'm hardly going to turn it down just to help you self-actualize, princess."

She opened her mouth in outrage. *"Princess?"*

A snatch of blues played and Christopher pulled out his cell phone. "Excuse me," he said, stepping away.

The voice that responded to his greeting was familiar. "Christopher, Dale White over at Pure Foods."

Dale White was the regional manager of the rapidly growing natural foods chain. Christopher took a deep breath, walking a few more steps away, trying to release his irritation. "Hey, Dale, how's it going?"

"Can't complain. How about yourself?"

"I'm good."

"I think you're about to be a whole lot better. Remember some of those roadblocks we've been running into with getting your chèvre into our stores? That might be changing here in a couple weeks."

"That's good news." Christopher managed—barely— to keep the cynicism out of his voice. He believed that Dale honestly wanted to buy his product, but he'd lost count of the number of conversations they'd had over the previous six months, trying to make it happen. Dale always predicted success, and the result was always more delay.

"What's the deal?" Christopher asked now, studying a gap where he had hoped to build a new shed before the snow started falling.

"Well, the organization has just announced an 'Eat Local' initiative. Beginning in a few weeks, regional managers will be tasked with buying at least a quarter of their fresh meat, dairy and produce from local sources."

That got his attention. "Twenty-five percent?"

"Yep."

It was worth getting excited about, assuming it was real. "Are regional managers going to have the authority to cut supply agreements?"

"Once the paperwork gets cleared up, yeah. I can't guarantee that it'll be right away, but the wheels are turning. I've got the announcement right here in my hands."

"If there's one thing I've learned in this business, Dale, it's that there is no such thing as a guarantee."

"This is as close as you'll get to one, my friend."

The question was would it be close enough? Christopher wondered as he disconnected. More important, would it happen in time? But he felt the grin spread across his face nonetheless. It wasn't a guarantee, but it was hope. And he could use all the hope he could get just then.

Carter Hayes's offer to prop up the farm's finances in order to keep it running long enough for him to learn the ropes was a solution but one Christopher had been growing less comfortable with by the day. The Pure Foods deal might get him out of that.

He glanced over at Larkin who stood, arms folded, foot tapping. And it might get him something else. Wiping away his smile, he approached her. "Sorry about that. Big doings on the goat herder network."

"I'm sure."

"So where were we?"

"The bet. Are you in or out?"

She stared him down. Feisty didn't begin to cover it. The idea of showing her what his life was truly like appealed to him. But it was more than that. There was unfinished business between them. Maybe her bet presented a way to kill two birds with one stone. He ran his tongue along his teeth and shook his head.

"Have you ever even done any manual labor in your life?"

Larkin raised her chin. "I don't think it's any of your business. What matters is the bet. If you're so sure I'm going to pancake, what's holding you up? Go ahead. Say yes if you're so sure you're right."

"But there's a lot at stake here—at least if you win. What if you lose? What do I get?"

She gave an impatient shake of her head. "Whatever you want, it doesn't matter. I don't intend to lose."

His smile grew broader. "So let me get this straight. You say you'll work the farm, whatever I ask, whatever the hours, no complaints?"

"No complaints."

"Not even to the goats?"

"Not to anyone. Whatever you want, for two weeks."

"For a month," he countered.

"A mo—" She stared at him.

"I've got a lot to lose," he said reasonably. "You do a month and you've got my word I'll walk away from Carter's money. Not that I have anything to worry about because I don't think for a minute you'll do it," he added.

"Fine." She glared at him. "When do we start?"

He glanced down at her miniskirt and stocking-covered feet, lips twitching. "How about now?"

Chapter Ten

"The diamond studs make the look," Christopher said.

Larkin scowled. "Very funny."

She still wore the Governator T-shirt, tucked into a pair of what she was certain were Christopher's oldest jeans, cinched in so the waistband crumpled around her hips like a paper bag. On her feet, currently padded in three pairs of socks, were cracked gum boots stained with God only knew what. She'd pulled her hair back and slipped on some beat-up gloves he'd unearthed. It was about as good as it was going to get.

"Ready to go?" he asked, and set off without waiting for her answer.

It wasn't the first time her temper had gotten her in trouble. Never this deep, though. The bucolic country life sounded all well and good, but she'd always been happy to leave the dirt and barnyards and animals to someone else.

That was about to change.

They heard them before they saw them, a chorus of bleats sounding from above. As she and Christopher stepped into the pasture, they appeared. Tan and brown, fawn and white and brindle, the goats hurried over the crest of the hill, looking bony, ungainly and purposeful…and oddly endearing, she realized. They had triangular faces with wide eyes, pointy noses and floppy ears that hung down on either side of their heads like dreadlocks. Their stumpy little tails wagged madly as they streamed down the hill, bouncing sideways with excitement.

Up close, they were bigger than she'd expected, coming to mid-thigh on her. They wore tagged collars like pets, but the sheer numbers were overwhelming enough to make her tense as they approached. Then they were there, swarming around, shoving past, jostling one another for position, and as she stood in the sea of goats, some of her nerves began to ease. They didn't care about her, she realized. They had a more important objective.

Christopher.

Of course, she thought. They were girls.

"I see you've been using your charm on them."

"I've got natural charisma, what can I tell you? Okay, guys, come on, new pasture," he said, walking to a metal gate.

Having learned her lesson, Larkin kept her hands off the wire. An imperious-looking white goat pushed to the front to be the first one through when Christopher opened the gate. The rest of the herd streamed through after her. From the leader's chin dangled a silky white lock of hair the length of Larkin's hand.

"I thought only billy goats had beards," she exclaimed.

"Bucks, not billy goats," he corrected. "And don't stare, she'll get self conscious. It's not Gilda's fault she's got a facial hair problem."

"Gilda?"

"She's the alpha goat."

"I thought the lead goat was supposed to have a bell."

"You're thinking of a cow," he said. "Gilda isn't worried about leading anyone anywhere. Her priority is just getting there first."

"She's good at it."

"Oh, she runs the show. No one messes with her unless they want to be butted through a wall."

"Butted through a—" Larkin felt a bump at her leg. She jumped and whirled around to see a little buff-colored goat with brown ears and a foolishly tiny mouth. The wide-eyed, triangular face inspected her, then sniffed at her hands and nibbled experimentally.

"She wants to see if you're good to eat," Christopher said. "Don't you, Tallulah?"

"Tallulah?"

"Larkin was already taken."

"I'm not nearly as tasty as grass." Larkin scratched behind Tallulah's ears. The little goat's eyes closed beatifically, and she bumped her head against Larkin. "Oh," she said in surprised pleasure. "You like that, don't you?"

"Looks like you've made a friend," Christopher said. "She needs one. She's small, so she gets pushed around a little."

"That's not very nice of them, is it, Tallulah?" Larkin asked. Tallulah made a little grumbling noise of agreement.

"Theda gets after her pretty good."

"Theda?"

"Bara." He pointed to a gray goat with white-speckled ears.

"What's her name?" She nodded at a camel-colored goat with lighter streaks running down her face.

"Mabel."

"And that one?"

"Bette," he replied instantly, scratching Mabel's ears.

"Bette?"

"Davis," he said as the doe gave a long, moaning bleat. "She's our diva."

If she hadn't still been annoyed with him, she'd have been amused. "Do you know all of them individually?"

"Well, yeah. I raised them. We wean them almost immediately so I bottle-feed them."

"Mr. Mom?"

He grinned. "So to speak. I started out with ten goats when I bought the place."

"And you have a hundred now? What are they, half rabbit?"

"Well, Spike and Mike and Leroy are, shall we say, enthusiastic about their jobs."

"Spike and Mike and Leroy?"

"The bucks. I keep them up on the top pasture," he added. "They've got their own shed, although they're scrappy enough that no coyote with any sense is going to mess with them. But you'll want to keep your distance."

"Why? Will they chase me?"

"No, they're usually pretty easy to be around, unless you want to push them somewhere they don't want to go. Otherwise, they want to make friends, but that's kind of the problem."

"Why's that?"

"They reek."

She rolled her eyes. "Charming."

"The does think so."

"I'd like to think Tallulah has better taste." Larkin rubbed the neck of the little goat, who still leaned against her.

"Maybe you're right. It looks like she's in love already," Christopher observed. "You're a natural as a goat herder."

"Carter always said I'd find my niche someday," she said dryly.

* * *

The cheese room, or the make room, as Christopher called it, could have doubled as an O.R., Larkin thought, staring around at the gleaming white tile floor, the pristine stainless steel counters. They wore white gowns and caps, sterile slippers on their feet. Looking at Christopher, she could see what he might look like as a surgeon.

But instead of checking a heart monitor, he stared at a thermometer that showed the temperature of milk in a four-foot-wide stainless-steel vat. Nodding to himself, he poured a bit of something into it.

"What did you just do?"

"Added rennet. It makes it coagulate. Take the paddle and give it a quick stir," he directed.

And as she did, before her astounded eyes, the texture of the milk began to change, magically thickening.

Christopher had joked with her once about food coming from the grocery store, but she'd never really thought about how it came to her plate. Cheese was something that just showed up on her salad, or on nachos. There was something fascinating about seeing the process from the beginning.

"What happens now?" she asked, raising the paddle out of the vat.

"It needs to sit for about an hour to finish coagulating. That's okay though. It gives us time to get the chèvre I made yesterday into the drying room."

He turned to a covered rack behind him and pulled out an oversize aluminum tray crowded with little plastic molds. One by one, he began extracting the cheeses, flipping the molds onto the work surface with a snap to release the little pyramids of chèvre inside, and setting them in turn on fresh trays.

Larkin reached out to grab one.

Christopher opened his mouth. "Don't—"

But she'd already flipped the mold over, thumping it down on the counter like Christopher had. Or not exactly—only the bottom part came out. The top part of the pyramid remained inside the mold.

"Whoops," she said.

"That would retail for about four dollars." His words came out clipped. "I think the agreement was that you do whatever I say, not whatever you want."

"I didn't mean to—"

"But you did. Each time you cart off and do something without being told, it'll cost you five bucks."

Larkin's mouth opened in outrage. "Five bucks? That's—"

He waited. "Yes?"

She subsided. "Nothing."

"Good. Just so you know, that's special for you. If it was anybody else it would be a quarter."

"I was only trying to help," she said sulkily.

"You can do that by listening. There's stuff you can do right off the bat and stuff that takes time to learn. It takes patience. You'll get to it eventually." He gave her a mocking look. "Assuming you stick around. For now, I'm going to take these into the drying room. See all the molds? Take them to the sink in the cheese room. They need to be cleaned."

"By me?"

"You see anyone else around? Deke's out working the fence lines."

"Where will you be?" she asked.

"I need to go turn the cheese in the cheese cave."

"The cheese cave?"

He nodded. "If you're good, I'll show it to you tomorrow."

"What about now?"

"Now you need to clean molds."

At home, she went to restaurants. She had a housekeeper, not to mention an automatic dishwasher. "I thought the job was cheesemaking, not washing up."

"Are you kidding? Ninety percent of what we do around here is washing up. Cleaning and sterilizing."

"Great."

"Is that a complaint?"

She moved her jaw around. "Of course not. I was just saying great because of…because I really like washing pans."

There was a definite light of amusement in his eyes, she thought in annoyance. "Good, because you know what complaining means."

"You're enjoying this, aren't you?" she asked.

"Of course. Do you blame me?"

She glowered at him. "Where's the soap?"

"In the cabinet over your head. There are some rubber gloves there, too, in case you're worried about your manicure." He winked at her. "Have fun."

She stuck out her tongue at his retreating back.

"So what does cutting wood have to do with making chèvre?"

Larkin looked over at Christopher from the clearing where he was splitting sections of log.

"Keeping the farm going has to do with making chèvre, and cutting wood has to do with keeping the farm going. Fuel for winter. Wood for the meat smoker." He grunted as he brought the ax down. The split wood fell down to either side, and Larkin leaned in to pick it up. "Some of it, I leave as logs to turn into lumber for new buildings. Some of it, I sell."

She stacked the wood on the cart Christopher had driven out from the barn, as she had been doing for over an hour. Christopher, meanwhile, just kept going with no sign of fatigue, moving easily, muscles flexing and tightening, wielding chainsaw and ax like they were weightless.

Not that she was watching him, or anything.

"Aren't you getting tired?" she asked.

"No. Are you?"

"Of course not," she lied.

He brought the ax down. "Good, because I'd hate to see you lose the bet on the first day."

Larkin picked up more wood. "You're not going to see me lose the bet at all."

The sun had moved well over in the sky by the time he finished cutting up the last log. She'd signed on for goats and cheesemaking, Larkin thought, not lessons in being a lumberjack. Still, a bet was a bet and she was damned well going to win it.

That didn't keep her from thinking fondly about taking a break when they got back. Something to drink, a chance to just sit. Her back and feet were killing her. But they'd finished with the cheese, and the make room was spic and span. They just needed to give the pigs and chickens their dinners and they'd be done. One day down, thirty to go, she thought smugly.

"All right, done with that. Let's get back and do the feeding," Christopher said. "We should have just enough time to get the cart unloaded before we have to get the goats in for milking."

Larkin blinked. "Milking? Don't you do that in the morning?"

"Twice a day every day. We wouldn't want to get bored."

"Of course not." She could practically see her fantasy of a cool glass of wine evaporating.

Instead, she found herself standing in the pasteurization room with Christopher. Pipes came through the wall from the milking parlor to form a bewildering maze up at the ceiling. "The milk comes in through the pipes and goes into this vat," Christopher said. "But first, we need to sterilize."

"Ninety percent of the job," she muttered, her heart sinking.

"Sometimes ninety-five. Cheer up, though. This time around, it's automatic."

And then he started manipulating the pipes, unscrewing some, tilting them or hanging them from hooks, connecting them to others. At first she tried to follow what he was doing. Then she just gave up and watched helplessly. Finally, she stood, arms folded across her chest. "You don't really expect me to remember that, do you?"

"Of course. You watched it once. That should be enough."

"Oh, sure, piece of cake," she said.

Grinning, he screwed a small jar of sterilizing solution into the bottom of a pipe and pressed a switch. Instantly, Larkin heard the sound of rushing water and the pipes began to shudder alarmingly. "It's recirculating to clean the pipes." Christopher turned toward the milking parlor. "Of course, that's if you do it right." He glanced back over his shoulder. "You hook it up wrong, you sterilize the floor instead."

"Good to have one more thing to worry about."

The milking parlor was another tile-lined room, this time with a concrete floor. Projecting out from the far wall were two long, raised blue metal platforms, each surrounded by vertical rails. As much as anything, they looked like a pair of long pens on stilts.

"The milking stands," Christopher said. "The does come through those trapdoors in the wall and put their heads between the stanchions to eat. We lock them in place, then go down that little aisle in between to put on the inflators to milk them."

He pointed to a maze of clear plastic tubes that hung from the railings on the inner aisle, feeding back to another maze of pipes that ran along the floor and over to the corner, into a round glass sphere the size of a beach ball. Pipes from there went up and over into the pasteurization room.

"Is this a goat milking room or chemistry lab?" Larkin asked.

"A little of both. The sterilizer needs to run for a few more minutes. Come on, let's go get the girls."

The goat barn was partitioned into sawdust-lined pens maybe sixteen feet on a side, all connected to a back passageway that ran along the side of the barn to the door that would let them in. On the front side of the pens ran a metal grate of slanting bars with a concrete-floored open area before it.

"Help me move that gate," Christopher directed. It created a little passageway to yet another door.

"What's this for?"

"When the does are milked out, they come out of the milking parlor and through this door to the holding pen outside. In the mornings, we take them out to pasture. At night, we bring them back into the pens to sleep."

"You're very organized."

"I've got to be," he said.

Larkin stood on the concrete, studying the green tractor that sat in a corner. In the loft above the pens, hay bales were stacked.

Christopher ran lightly up a ladder. "Watch out," he called as he forked down a bale and swung down. "Scatter hay along the concrete in front of the feeding grate. I'll go let them in."

He disappeared for a moment, then she heard bleats and the staccato thud of hooves. The herd came skidding and racing pell-mell around the corner, Gilda in the lead. Rushing up to the metal fence, they jammed their heads through to begin gobbling the hay as though they expected it to be snatched away any moment.

In a matter of minutes, the grid was a solid line of goats, shoulder to shoulder, munching industriously. She saw Gilda and a goat that she thought was Mabel, and even Bette Davis, but one seemed to be missing.

Larkin finished scattering the alfalfa and walked up the row, searching for a buff-colored head. And then she saw her, trying vainly to squeeze between two other goats to get to the food. "Here, Tallulah," she called. The little goat looked up. Larkin shook a handful of hay. "Down here."

Tallulah scrambled down to the end where Larkin tossed the alfalfa down before her. And maybe it was just Larkin's imagination but she swore that she saw a glimmer of gratefulness in Tallulah's eyes before the little goat tucked in.

"Tallulah's got a friend."

Larkin whirled to find Christopher standing behind her, a half smile on his face. "Well, the other goats weren't letting her in," she said awkwardly.

He brushed a fingertip over her chin. "Nice."

And she felt goose bumps rise on her arms. "I am nice. At least to the ones who deserve it, like Tallulah."

"I'll keep that in mind," he said. "Now, let's go milk."

In the pasteurization room, he went through another bewildering process of rearranging pipes to ensure the milk would go to the right place.

Larkin watched him, hands on her hips. "Do you really need to move all those pipes or are you shuffling some of them around just so I'll screw it up when it's my turn?"

"What do you think?"

She eyed him. "I wouldn't put anything past you."

"Cynic."

"Realist."

In the milking parlor, they hung individual feed bins on

the outside of the blue platforms. "Grain goes in before the does get here, always," he said. "That's important." A series of thumps emanated from the trapdoors between the milking stands and the barn.

Larkin frowned. "What's that?"

"That would be Gilda and the girls, telling us to get our acts in gear."

It charmed her. "They want to get in? Do they like being milked?"

He grinned. "They like to eat. As long as we bribe them with food, they'll stand still for whatever else we want to do. Kind of like people."

"Cynic."

"Realist. Okay, we're sterilized, hooked up and clean. We just need a little music and we're in business." He turned and began sorting through a stack of CDs in front of a boom box.

"The goats like music?"

"Love it. Won't milk without it." He pulled out a CD. "They're big blues and classic rock fans. Hate classical."

"You don't say." Larkin stuck her tongue in her cheek as Stevie Ray Vaughan filled the room. "I don't suppose you're a big blues and classic rock fan, are you?"

He flicked her an amused glance. "Me? No way, I'm a Mozart man through and through." He reached for the rope that raised the trapdoors. The minute he did, Gilda scrambled through onto one milking stand, followed by at least a half dozen more does before Christopher lowered the door. Mabel led the charge on the other side. The goats stuck their heads through the stanchions to the feed bins and started munching, flipping their tails in excitement.

Larkin shook her head, mystified. "But they've just spent the past fifteen minutes eating in the barn."

"That was the salad course." Christopher moved the bars that locked their heads in place. "This is the entrée."

She followed him into the aisle between the two milking stands and found herself staring at two rows of goat backsides. "All right, first, we sterilize, to keep the girls healthy." He walked down the row with a neoprene beaker of iodine, dipping each teat. "Now, we strip out any old milk by hand." He got a metal cup.

"We?"

"We," he said firmly. "Make the okay sign."

Mystified, she did.

"Now, make an okay around the top of the teat. Squeeze at the top and then squeeze your other fingers."

She reached out tentatively. The goat's flank was smooth, the udder warm.

"Come on," Christopher encouraged. "Don't be scared. This is Mabel, she's pretty tame. I won't make you do Gilda." As though she heard, Gilda stamped a back leg.

Mabel munched quietly, taking a bite and looking back over her shoulder as though to ask what was taking so long. Larkin took a breath and made the okay sign. She squeezed, and in triumph saw the milk shoot out into the cup. "I did it!" she cried.

She'd been all around the world. She'd met celebrities, been in magazines, even made it into a feature film as a bit player. Who knew she could get excited about milking a goat?

"Good girl," Christopher said, working his way down the rest of the row. "Now do the other teat. Done? Okay, then we just put on the inflators." He slipped clear plastic tubes over the goat's teats, and milk began shooting out immediately, running through the plastic tubes to shoot into the clear beach-ball sphere.

"Look at that," she exclaimed, lips curving.

"Trust me, after you do it twice a day for five years, it's infinitely less exciting."

"No wow factor?"

He looked at her. "Sometimes," he said. "Sometimes, there's definitely a wow."

The seconds stretched out as they looked at each other. Almost imperceptibly he leaned in toward her.

A thump on the other side of the door had Larkin jumping. She flushed. "Don't you have goats to milk?"

"They think so," he said.

"Well, let's get to it. Tallulah's waiting."

She had never been so tired in her entire life. Never. Ever. It seemed like weeks had gone by since she'd arrived at the farm, and for every minute of that time they'd been going. She climbed the kitchen steps on leaden feet, stumbling in the doorway.

Christopher grabbed her. "Watch out."

She yawned. "That requires having my eyes open. I was on the red-eye last night, remember?"

"Where are you staying?"

"Oh, hell," she said blankly.

He raised a brow. "Is that new?"

"Funny. I forgot all about it. There's got to be a place around here that has an open room, though. Where's the nearest hotel?"

"Montclair, but you're in no shape to be driving there right now."

"Fine." She yawned again. "I'll sleep in the car."

He shook his head and took the bag of clothes from her hand. "Come on."

"What?"

"You're staying here."

"Doing anything you tell me doesn't include that," she retorted.

"In my guest room, not my bed. Trust me, I don't make

a habit of molesting unconscious women." His teeth gleamed. "It's much more interesting when you're awake."

She tried to give him a hard stare but spoiled it with a jaw-cracking yawn. "All right. Just promise me I can take a shower."

"Assuming you can keep your eyes open, you can have all the hot water you can take."

Chapter Eleven

She'd been at it forever, Larkin thought. No sooner did she milk out one group of goats than she heard the others butting against the trapdoor to get in. "I'm going as fast as I can," she told them, hurrying to open the gates on the far ends of the milking stands to let the finished goats hop down and circle back outside through the passageway.

Not that her words meant anything to the ones on the ramp to the trapdoors. They wanted in and they wanted it now, and they weren't shy about letting her know. It just seemed like the faster she tried to go, the further behind she found herself. "I'm trying," she said again, working to untangle the tubing and inflators that went on the udders. The thuds against the wall were more insistent now, the wood creaking with every butt.

Then she looked up and saw that the trapdoors were gone, that there was only a smooth wall that now shuddered with the force of the entire herd, straining and splintering, the pounding louder and louder and louder....

Larkin swam reluctantly up out of sleep to an insistent knocking on the door. "G'way," she muttered.

For a moment, it stopped, and then sudden light shone through her eyelids.

"Come on, princess, time to get up."

Larkin groaned. It was Christopher. Her initial impulse to murder him was mitigated both by the fact that it would require opening her eyes and the fact that her arms were almost too sore to raise.

"I can't move," she groaned. "I must have torn a muscle yesterday."

"You probably did lots of things to your muscles if my memory of the first day on the farm is anything to go by," he said cheerfully. "Come on, get up. I brought you coffee. The sooner you get moving, the sooner the stiffness will go away." He tossed something on the foot of her bed.

"What's that?" she muttered bad-temperedly.

"Jeans, a clean T-shirt, some more socks." When she dragged a pillow over her head, he pulled it away. Out in the yard, she heard the crow of a rooster; behind it, a peremptory and ever-swelling chorus of goat bleats.

"Come on," Christopher said. "We've got to get cracking. If we're not out there in fifteen minutes, they're going to start taking the place down."

"Where's Deke?"

"Taking care of the pigs." He gave her a speculative glance. "What are you wearing under there, anyway?"

She pulled the covers to her chin. "Don't get any ideas, buster," she said. "I'm not looking for company."

"Good." He reached out and yanked the covers down. Larkin yelped.

"There's a clean towel and a new toothbrush in the

bathroom," he said as he walked out the door, then stuck his head back in. "Nice legs."

Her response was a choice name.

"No complaining," he said through the door.

"That wasn't a complaint," she grouched back. "It was a statement of fact."

At least he'd brought coffee. She reached out and took a swallow then stood in the oversize gray Georgetown University T-shirt that she'd slept in. When she bent to pick up the clothes off the bed, she gave a surprised groan. She was sore in places she'd never thought about before. "Sadist," she muttered.

"I heard that," Christopher said through the door, then his footsteps thumped down the stairs.

He'd finished reading the news on his laptop by the time Larkin stumbled down to the kitchen.

"Coffee."

He pointed to the percolator. "Help yourself. You look like you're moving a little better."

"I've never been so sore my life."

"Bad time to quote Nietzsche, I suppose."

She scowled.

"There are eggs on the stove and bagels next to it," he said. Better not to tell her that the second day was always the worst, he figured. Best to let her find it on her own.

Instead, he watched her make her bleary-eyed way over to the table. He thumped down a thick catalog in front of her.

She forked up some eggs. "What's that?"

"Breakfast reading," he said. "L.L. Bean. Farm-ready fashion. They can overnight you whatever you want."

"Wouldn't it be better for me to just drive to the nearest store and buy something?" she asked hopefully.

"Nope. We've got to milk."

"After that," she said.

"Then we've got the farmers' market from nine to two." He rose to pour himself some more coffee.

"The farmers' market?"

"Sure. There's no point in making cheese if we don't sell it. Scarf up. We've got to milk and get over there by eight so we can set up."

She looked at him for a moment. "Are you sure there's nothing you need at L.L. Bean that I can go buy?"

"Not unless you're prepared to lose the bet." He waited, then nodded to himself. "I didn't think so. Five minutes and we start milking."

"But I have to order clothes," she protested.

"They're open twenty-four hours a day. Order tonight. You can borrow more of my stuff for tomorrow."

She swallowed another bite and gave him a look from under her brows. "You know, workers are required by law to get two breaks and a lunch in a day. Probably double that if they get forced to work fourteen hours straight."

He raised a brow. "Is that a complaint?"

"Statement of fact. I'm telling you for your own protection." She finished her eggs and rose to take her plate to the sink. "I'd hate to see you in violation of the labor code."

"So, what are you, one of those union agitators?" he asked in amusement.

She leaned against the counter, arms folded. "The International Brotherhood of Goat Milkers will never rest until its workers are treated fairly."

Brotherhood? One thing she was not, he thought, watching her slender form at the sink, was anything close to male. "You know, that sounded very close to complaining."

"Not at all. I'm just appealing to your enlightened self-interest. You keep the workers happy, you'll get happy goats, and you know what they say, happy goats give happy cheese."

"I see." He walked over to rinse out his coffee cup. "And are you going to tell me my goats' happiness requires shopping? Or a 10:00 a.m. start time?"

"Nothing so extreme," she said with dignity. "All we ask is that the workers are allowed to satisfy their most basic needs. A short lunch break to nibble a crust of bread and buy some rags to toil in."

He eyed the catalog. "Rags?"

"Possibly fleece," she admitted.

"I'll tell you what. I'll go get the milking started so you can buy your rags—"

"Great," she began.

"—and in return, you cook."

"Cook?" Larkin squeaked.

"Yeah. Dinner, ever heard of it?"

"Well, yeah, but—"

"But nothing. You're supposed to do whatever I tell you, remember?"

"On the farm," she qualified.

He gestured toward the window, which overlooked the barnyard. "Looks like we're on the farm to me."

"I'm your guest."

"No, you're my intern. And I cooked last night. You're up." He rose. "I like goat cheese."

They'd named it wrong, Larkin thought. The farmers' market wasn't so much a market as a festival. Dozens of colorful tarps pitched in tidy rows transformed what had been an empty field into a shopper's bazaar. Vendors offering tomatoes and peppers and squash sat side by side with others selling jewelry or purses or handwoven rugs.

To one side, a masseur set out his massage chair. On a stage, a guitar and drum duo tuned up their instruments.

Beyond was the best part of the market as far as Larkin was concerned: a row of stands selling prepared food, savory scents already rising from them. If nothing else, she would get lunch.

Some of the vendors went for a more established look, putting up wood frame and fiberglass shelters. For every sign made of poster board and magic marker, there were more stylish versions in wood and metal that would have been equally at home in front of a boutique. This wasn't just a bunch of growers selling bushel baskets of peaches out of the backs of their trucks; the farmers' market was a serious business.

Christopher eschewed the built-in type shelter in favor of a bright blue tarp and a table with a cloth hanging over the front carrying the Doe Si Doe Farm logo. Of course, he had one other thing the other booths didn't have—he had Tallulah.

"She's my goodwill ambassador," he said. "And she'll keep you company. You two have gotten to be such good friends, I figure you'd miss her if you were gone too long."

He staked the little buff-colored goat on a leash a few feet away from the booth, with her own dish of water. It took Tallulah approximately five seconds to look at the grass around her and decide that she'd been taken out for a gourmet meal—she went to work enthusiastically while Christopher and Larkin unpacked everything else.

"Okay, the health department is very serious about the hand sanitizer and the rubber gloves," Christopher said, "and I'm very serious about the health department, so be sure to use them both."

He set out jugs of maple syrup and jars of something

called maple butter, all of them marked Trask Farms. "Is that Jacob's?" Larkin asked.

He nodded. "And my aunt Molly's. I trade off weeks with them. Makes more sense to share a booth between us than pay for two."

He started setting out the cheese, each round or pyramid neatly sealed in plastic with a Doe Si Doe label. There were dozens of them. "When did you find time to do all this?" Larkin asked.

He put out dishes of dried fruit and nuts. "Last night, after you crashed."

Which would have made it nine o'clock, at the earliest, she thought, watching him put out maple candy. His hands were quick, capable. She already knew how strong they were.

And how clever.

Not that she needed to be thinking about that. She was there to win a bet, nothing more. Still... "I could have helped."

He shrugged. "I figured you needed sleep more."

"If you were up after I went to bed, you work a pretty long day."

"Goes with the territory," he said. "Of course, now that you're around, there'll be more hands. You can help with the wrapping and shipping."

"Why don't you have Deke pitch in?"

"Same reason I don't bring him here. Deke's good with the stock and general farm stuff. He's not so great with people."

"Or cheese?"

Christopher nodded. "He freezes up with anything requiring precision. Used to have a pretty serious drinking problem, I guess. He dried out a few years back, around the time my herd was getting pretty good sized. I figured I'd give him a go and see what happened."

Deke hadn't had much of a track record, and yet Christopher had looked beyond that. "You took a chance on him. A lot of people wouldn't have."

He ducked down to rummage around in the coolers. Almost as though he were embarrassed, she thought. "People deserve a chance to change. And anyway, it's worked out. He's been steady for me. The does like him. The only reason I was able to go on that cruise was because Deke was home taking care of the place."

"As hard as you go at it, I'm kind of surprised you were able to leave even with Deke. When was the last time you had a vacation?"

"The year before I bought the farm. I went to the south of France. It was kind of what got me thinking about the whole thing."

Went alone or with someone? Not that it was any of her business, she reminded herself. Not that she cared. "I'd say after five years of this, you had a vacation coming."

"I hadn't planned it. The Alaska trip all came up by accident. My cousin Nick and his wife got pregnant and she couldn't fly, so all of a sudden there was a spare room. Otherwise, I wouldn't have been there."

How different it would all have been. No laughing faces to help her and Carter reach out to one another, no company on the glacier.

No kiss on the fantail.

It didn't matter, Larkin reminded herself impatiently. By all rights, she ought to have been in L.A. at that moment, not standing in a grassy field by a river, watching the first customers trickle in. L.A. was the real world, the life she'd chosen. This was just an interlude, and she'd be smart to remember it.

Christopher set out a board with a glass dome. One by one, he unwrapped cheeses and set them on it. "The best way to sell is to give people a taste. We've got feta, an aged goat cheese that's closer to brie, pyramids of plain chèvre and a chèvre with roasted garlic and tarragon."

She glanced at him. "Garlic tarragon? Getting a little fancy, aren't you?"

Instead of answering, he spread a bit of the plain chèvre on a cracker. "You should know what you're selling. Here, try it."

It had the expected tang of goat cheese, yet it was smoother, somehow, almost silky. But she only registered it in passing because what she really noticed, what every nerve in her body was focused on, was the way his fingers had brushed against her lips as he fed her the morsel. Like some sort of silent gong had been struck, she felt awareness vibrate through her.

Christopher watched her, holding another cracker. "Now, try the roasted garlic tarragon."

His fingertips brushed her cheek as he fed her. This time, the flavor was a complex mix of the cheese against the almost sweet mellowness of the roasted garlic and the licorice flavor of the tarragon. She licked her lips.

His eyes darkened. "And this is the brie type."

Rich and smooth, with a faint hint of tang, the flavor of the cheese spread through her mouth. But as his fingers lingered, that wasn't the flavor she wanted. She wanted the flavor of him, the feel of him, the crush of his mouth on hers. They couldn't kiss each other, standing there as the market was opening, she knew that. She shouldn't even want it. But his thumb rubbed across her lower lip. With the other hand, he brushed loose strands of hair from her face.

And slowly, watching her the whole time, he leaned in and pressed his lips to hers.

He could overwhelm her, she knew that. He could assault her senses until she was helpless to do anything but feel. He wasn't doing that now, though. He was merely cradling her face and touching his mouth to hers.

How was it that she felt it everywhere?

The moments crept by, utterly absorbing her. He changed the angle of the kiss, rubbed his lips against hers. When they parted, he didn't take it deeper. He didn't slide his arms around her and plunge her into hot arousal with the feel of that hard body of his. It was as though for all that lay between them, he knew he could bring her to surrender and, knowing that, could merely amuse himself by teasing her.

And then she felt the shudder run through him.

He raised his head, staring at her. "We keep winding up in public."

"I know."

"We need to change that."

Behind them, the metal tag on Tallulah's collar jingled. "The market's opening." Larkin fought to keep her voice steady.

"This isn't finished," he said, and released her.

Around them, the first customers were beginning to drift through the aisles. Larkin willed her system to settle. She wasn't here for romance. She was here to get Carter off the hook. Period.

A young woman wearing a Dartmouth T-shirt walked up. "I'd like a block of the herbed chèvre."

Pay attention, Larkin thought to herself.

The morning wore on, and with it came surprises. She hadn't been entirely sure that she'd do any better than Deke when it came to dealing with customers at the market, but as the tide of people started flowing in, she surprised herself. And Christopher, perhaps, who kept glancing over at her as she made sale after sale.

"When we were unpacking, I thought you'd brought way too much, but now I'm thinking that we're going to run out," Larkin told him.

"That's because you're doing too good a job of convincing people to buy more."

"I bet I could do more if you put me on commission," she suggested. "You know, incentivize me."

His eyes darkened. "Just what kind of incentive are you looking for?" he asked.

Breathe, she reminded herself.

"Mama, doggie." A little boy stood in front of Tallulah, pointing with a chubby finger.

Larkin relaxed and grinned. "She's not a dog. She's a goat. Her name is Tallulah. Can you say hi, Tallulah?"

He stared. "Tulah," he experimented.

Tallulah bleated, and the little boy screwed up his eyes and giggled. "Again," he demanded. Tallulah obliged, and he laughed and stamped his feet.

"Mama," he said again. "Tulah."

His mother, a brunette in shorts and sandals, handed Christopher some bills and put the cheese in her string bag. "I see, Nathan. Pretty goat."

"You can pet her if it's okay with your mom," Larkin said, glancing over at the woman, who nodded.

Larkin stroked Tallulah's shoulder, then a round-eyed Nathan followed suit. Tallulah, meanwhile, eyed the grass as if planning her next mouthful.

"Time to go, Nathan," his mother told him.

"I want," he said, reaching toward Tallulah even as he was being scooped up.

"No goats, not today."

"Bye-bye, Tulah," he cried, waving.

Christopher shook his head. "That's how it starts. You got the kid hooked. Now he'll grow up to be a penniless goat farmer."

"There are worse things," Larkin said, glancing over from where she knelt. "He could be—"

"Got any of that cheese for me?" a familiar voice asked.

"Hey, Aunt Molly," Christopher said.

Larkin turned, mouth ajar.

Molly Trask. She should've expected to see her sooner or later. After all, she'd known Molly lived there—they shared market space with Christopher. Somehow, though, Larkin had never really thought about what she would say to her. Or how she felt about her, for that matter. Certainly if there was a primary reason that Carter was leaving everything behind for Vermont, it was Molly Trask. In that sense, she was just one more in a long line of the women who had dominated Carter's attention since Larkin's mother had died. And yet...

And yet she couldn't help liking the woman, even if she found herself watching in dismay as Carter rolled along his usual path like an avalanche gathering speed.

She barely had room in her brain to hold all of her conflicting emotions for Christopher; she wasn't sure what to do about Molly.

Christopher handed change to his customer and turned to his aunt. "What are you doing here? You're supposed to be off today. It's our turn."

"I'm here as a shopper, not a worker. I thought I'd come see what they've got here that my garden doesn't," she said. "I don't grow goat cheese, for instance. Why don't you pick two or three out for me? I'm going to be having a dinner guest later next— Good Lord," she blurted as Larkin stood. "Larkin? Is that you?"

Larkin had never been one to blush a whole lot, so she

was at a loss to explain why it was exactly that she'd been turning beet-red approximately once an hour since meeting the Trask family. "Hi, Molly. Good to see you again." She patted Tallulah's warm side a final time and walked over.

"It's nice to see you again, too—although it's something of a surprise, I must admit. Does your father know you're here?"

"Not yet," Larkin said uncomfortably, washing her hands with sanitizer and pulling on a pair of gloves. She looked around desperately for distraction, but Christopher was taking care of the last two people in line. Which left her no excuses. "I hear Dad's been by to visit you."

At least she wasn't the only one who blushed, Larkin thought, watching Molly's cheeks tint. "Last week." She fiddled with the strap of her purse. "It was quite a surprise, too."

There was something endearing about Molly's awkwardness. "He seems very taken with the area," Larkin said. *And with you.* "At least he was when I spoke with him."

"Oh, he's making all sorts of talk about moving and farming," Molly said. "But I wouldn't take that too seriously. He's already established a life for himself in the city. Not that I'd discourage anyone from moving to Washington County—it's as beautiful as they come. I want to see Carter happy. I just don't know if our brand of happy is really what he wants for the long-term." She gave a little smile. "Maybe you can help him figure that out. Is that why you're here?"

Larkin blinked. She was accustomed to Carter's women having agendas. She was accustomed to feeling either lobbied or shoved out of the picture. She wasn't accustomed to them talking to her out of concern for Carter's best interests. And she definitely wasn't accustomed to having them actually understand what was going on.

"He seems happy," she said. Then again, he always did at this stage. "I just thought I'd come out and see him."

"And while Carter's in New York, isn't it lucky that you've run into Christopher?" The question was overly casual.

"I went to the farm looking for Carter," Larkin said. But had she? Or had it been Christopher the whole time?

A smile spread over Molly's face. "Well, it's nice to see that Christopher has some help." Her voice was warm. "He works too hard."

"Believe me, after two days of it I know exactly how hard."

"Where are you staying?"

"In the guest room," Christopher cut in.

"Oh, isn't it lovely? I stayed there when our houses were being fumigated. It's the prettiest room in the whole house, with that giant hydrangea below."

"Is that the plant with the blue flowers?" Larkin asked.

Molly's expression warmed even further to delight. "It is. It takes iron to make it that blue. I've been tending Christopher's garden for the past few years, but I can show you—"

"Here's your cheese, Aunt Molly," Christopher interrupted. "The market's closing in an hour, so make sure you leave yourself time to get all the way around."

Molly gave him a knowing glance. "Well, Larkin, I don't know how long you plan to be in town, but perhaps you and I could have lunch one day. I'd enjoy getting to know you a little better." She caught Larkin's hands in hers.

Larkin squeezed back. "I'd like that," she found herself saying, and meaning it.

"It was a pleasure to see you. Please come by and say hello any time. We're happy to have you here."

"I'm happy to be here," she said.

And found herself meaning that, too.

* * *

"What a place that was," Larkin said as they walked into the kitchen. "I couldn't believe everything they had. Is it always crowded like that?"

"Pretty much. It's got a pretty strong reputation at this point. People know that's where you go. It kind of feeds on itself."

"And you've got so many repeat customers. That must be a good feeling." She set the bag she carried on the table next to Christopher's.

"So what's for dinner?" He set the rest of the bags on the table and started to dig through them. "Body butter?" He looked at the label and then at Larkin. "I'm guessing that's not for putting on toast."

"There are certain necessities that L.L. Bean doesn't carry, you know," she said, taking the jar from him.

He put his hand in the bag again and pulled out a pale blue silk scarf with flowers embroidered on it. "Also not for dinner."

"It's for mental nutrition," she said.

"I see. And do we have anything for the more conventional kind of nutrition? Unless I'm mistaken, you spent the past half hour of the farmers market buying food for tonight, right?"

"Oh, yes," she said enthusiastically.

He watched as she pulled out cartons and aluminum take-out bins. "What is that?"

Her eyes glimmered. "Food."

"You were supposed to get stuff for dinner."

"Oh, I did. I got pad Thai, samosas, chicken penang and baklava. Oh, and some stuff for salads."

He shook his head. "No, you were supposed to get stuff to cook."

She folded her arms over her chest. "Did you or did you not send me out to buy food for dinner?"

"Yes, but I—"

"Did you, or did you not?"

Recognizing he was beat, he gave up. "Yes."

"Good. Here it is."

He couldn't help but be amused. "Have you ever cooked a meal in your entire life?"

Larkin glanced back from putting the cartons in the refrigerator and gave him a wide smile. "Takeout. I excel at cooking takeout. Now let's go milk."

Chapter Twelve

Christopher walked to the gate in the upper pasture, moving the temporary fence so that he could transfer part of the herd. Two pastures over, he saw Larkin wave as she opened the gate to let a different group of goats in. She stood back, then, her hair bright in the sunlight, watching Gilda lead the rush to grass.

He'd figured it would only take a couple of days to run Larkin off, a couple of days he'd expected to thoroughly enjoy. But she'd stuck with it for a week and a half. She'd jettisoned her couture shoes and skirts for head-to-toe practical jeans and T-shirts complemented by tough leather gloves and duck boots. And somehow even then, standing there, she managed to invest them with style.

He shook his head at himself.

If anyone had told him a month before that Larkin Hayes would work on his farm for the better part of two weeks without complaint, he would've thought they'd been in the sun too long. If anyone had told him a month before that she'd sleep under his roof for that time without ever being in his bed, he would have thought they were just plain nuts. Chivalry, apparently, was alive and well in Vermont.

Even if it did feel more like rocks in his belly.

The original plan had been for her to get a hotel, but somehow it just hadn't seemed to make any sense. The farm was here, and he had the space. Better for her to stay where she could tumble into bed, exhausted, in these early, difficult days when her body was still catching up with the demands she was putting on it. Better for her, anyway.

For him?

The wanting was a constant companion of his days and nights. He'd taken to staying up until well after she'd gone to bed, just to be sure he wouldn't catch a sleep-depriving glimpse of her in that pretty little robe she'd bought that looked like all he'd have to do was reach out and untie the sash and slide his hands inside to find her warm and willing and—

Current jolted through him. He jerked his hands back, cursing. Brilliant. The first rule of electrified fencing was to pay attention, not fantasize about making love to a woman. But it was hard not to think about this particular woman. From before sunrise to long after sunset, she worked beside him. With the stubbornness of the smallest kid in the herd, she doggedly refused to be left behind. If he could do something, then she insisted on doing it, too.

He'd made the bet thinking that they'd finish off the business between them. He hadn't reckoned on how much it would lighten his days. It was more than just having another pair of hands; it was the laughter, the buoyancy, the genuine delight that she brought to it all. Somehow, with her beside him, he found himself looking at the farm with a fresh eye, savoring each moment, looking forward to the day.

Best not to get too accustomed to it, though, he reminded himself as he watched her walk down the hill. She would be gone in a couple more weeks. He needed to remember that.

Manicurists, Larkin thought, *couldn't possibly be paid enough.* Granted, bending over goat feet for hours trimming their hooves was a bit different than putting on acrylic nails in a salon, but the basic principle was the same. Except that goats didn't give tips, of course, or tell stories about their boyfriends.

She walked across the barnyard rubbing her shoulders. They were tougher than they looked. Some, like Tallulah, were docile, enjoying the attention. Others, like Gilda, took three of them to get the job done, and still fought tooth and nail. Or hoof, as the case was.

After working on it three days running, Larkin found herself dreaming about curled-up pieces of nail. The worst part was, even with Deke pitching in, they still had at least another day of it to look forward to.

She heard that school playground yelp she'd wondered about her first day on the farm, the one that sounded like the high-pitched squeals of kids. The four-legged kind, she realized now, not human ones, milling around the little fenced-in meadow next to the pig barn. Larkin walked past and glanced at the chicken pen, checking that the waterer was full. And then out of the corner of her eye, she saw something go flying through the air above the high grass.

Larkin shook her head. Yes, she was tired, but not tired enough to be seeing things, and the thing she'd seen had looked distinctly like, well, an airborne kid.

Right.

She looked at the meadow directly. A moment later, she saw it again, a little black goat arcing over to land with a rustle in the grass. A beat or two after, she saw another.

"Good Lord," she murmured. And started laughing.

They were jumping from a big rock in the center of the pasture, for all the world like human children at a playground. The fact that the flat top of the rock was well above their heads only served to encourage them. As she watched, each kid scrambled up on the rock, savored high ground for a moment, then launched itself exuberantly into space. They flew through the air, posing with legs and head and tail, looking for all the world like freestyle skiers without the skis. And the extraordinary part, the part that had her laughing so hard her stomach hurt, was that they stood in line to do it. They didn't butt one another, they didn't shove, they didn't try to play king of the hill.

They took turns.

"They doing the X Games again?" Christopher asked from behind her.

Larkin wiped her eyes. "What did you do, train them?"

"No, this was all their idea. Rufus, there, is gold-medal caliber. I'm thinking of entering him this year in the real X Games." As they watched, a gray kid with white-streaked ears leapt off, splaying his legs out in all directions.

"It's like having your own little farm of comedians. Did you know they were like this when you started? Did your family raise them or something?"

He shook his head. "Not exactly. I was a town kid. My grandparents farmed, though. They lived in upstate New York, had a small herd of Jerseys until I was about thirteen. We used to go stay with them in the summers. Being around the animals was the best part."

"Why not cattle, then? Why goats?"

He took off his gloves and stuck them in a pocket. "I knew I wanted to make chèvre, and anyway, I figured goats would be easier to manage than cows just because they're smaller. I was pretty sure I was going to try to run the place with only one or two other people."

"Practical," she said.

"You've got to be if you want to stay alive in this business. But I also just like them," he admitted. "They're smart, enough to recognize their own names, some of them. And tough." He looked over to watch Rufus jettison himself from the rock, twisting in midair. "And they're a little bit screwy. That's probably what I like about them best of all. I left my truck door open one day while I was working on it. Some of the kids got loose, and next thing I knew, they were climbing up in the cab and looking out the window."

"Like third graders," she said and smiled. "Playing on the playground."

"First graders," he corrected. "I finally had to take a saw to all the trees in that meadow, cut off the extra limbs so there weren't any crotches. Otherwise, it seemed like every day I'd go out and there'd be a kid stuck somewhere, looking at me like, 'Hey, buddy, over here.'"

Larkin laughed at the image. "So they're not always smart."

"You know any kids who are? They're like the joker you went to school with who did crazy stuff for the pure damn fun of it."

She watched the light in his eyes and felt a little tug of an emotion she couldn't quite identify. This farm, this life was a part of him. For all that in Alaska he'd spoken about how he only rarely thought to appreciate it, she'd seen the deep affection he had for his farm and his work. And his animals. They were individuals to him, each and every one.

Then again, with the goats, that was easy.

"I can see why you get such a kick out of them," she said. "They're such characters."

"Absolutely. They know who they are, and they're not afraid to tell you about it. Kind of like people but more fun."

"Now that's odd," she mused. "I had you picked for an extrovert. I mean, how did you spend all those years in Washington without being a people person?" How had he spent all that time there, period?

"Maybe all those years in Washington are exactly why I'm not a people person anymore."

She couldn't imagine him making the rounds, with a slick haircut and an even slicker smile. How had that person turned into the man who stood before her? She shook her head. "It's funny, I've always sort of assumed that people don't really ever change once they're grown."

"I think they can, if it's their choice. Or if something happens. I did it, Deke did it, maybe your father's trying to do it, too. I think anyone who thinks they're going to change someone else is dreaming, but, yeah, I think we all ultimately decide who we're going to be."

"And you decided to be a gentleman goat farmer."

His teeth gleamed. "I'm moving up in your book. A couple weeks ago, I was a goatherd."

"You know—" Larkin stopped.

"What?"

"I never meant it like that." She met his gaze. "I wasn't trying to insult you."

In the meadow, the kids had abandoned the X Games for king of the hill. Cicadas buzzed in the trees. Christopher nodded slowly. "I shouldn't have taken it so seriously," he said. "It wasn't how I wanted that evening to end."

Simple words, and yet they had her pulse thudding a little harder. For all that they butted heads as often as the goats, there was this thing that still hummed between them, beneath every word they spoke to each other, every glance, every breath. Always in her mind was the awareness, the speculation.

The want.

"I wonder," she began.

"So do I." He reached out and hooked his finger in one of her belt loops, tugging her closer. "I wonder a lot. I wonder what it would be like if we ever once found ourselves in a quiet, private place. I wonder what it would be like to make love with you in the light, where I could spend hours touching every inch of your body."

The words dried up in her throat. The background noises faded. All she could hear was the sound of her own breath. All she could feel was the warmth of his hands, sliding over her hips. And all she could think of was what it would be like to be naked against him as they became one.

Deke was around, Christopher reminded himself. Once again, it wasn't the place or the time. He tried to dial back the desire that had become a steady ache, a regular companion to his days and nights. It simply wasn't possible. They could go inside, he thought feverishly, lowering his face to hers. Just once, he could say to hell with it and let the myriad little tasks remain undone for one day. In five minutes, they could be upstairs, naked and feasting on each other. In five minutes, she could be his.

A horn startled them as a car crunched up the gravel drive. Christopher looked over and cursed. And released her immediately.

"Who's that?" Larkin asked.

"Looks like Carter's back."

* * *

"*In*tern?" Carter repeated as he and Larkin walked into the kitchen.

"It's a long story," she muttered.

Carter looked at her from under his brows. "Trust me, I've got time." He walked to the table and pulled out a chair.

Larkin had seen his face when he'd driven up; she'd seen the shock written all over it. Molly, apparently, hadn't said a word about her being there. Her respect for the Trask matriarch rose another notch.

"Can I get you something to drink?" she asked. "Water or coffee?"

"Coffee." He watched as she rose to make it, not missing the self-assured way she moved around the kitchen. "You've been here for a while." It wasn't phrased as a question.

Larkin shrugged. "A week and a half, maybe more." Had it been only that? It seemed so very much longer. Real life back in Los Angeles had faded away, replaced by labor, laughter, by so many new experiences she couldn't count them all. She suppressed the flicker of uneasiness. "I think I got here just after you left."

"You didn't waste any time."

"I was concerned. I was hoping to talk to you."

"About what? As if I didn't know."

She'd flown across the continent with emotions roiling, arguing with him in her head. Now, all these days later, what she wanted to say was far less clear. "I suppose I had the impression that after divorcing Celine, you were going to take a little bit of time and figure things out," she said finally, as the coffee machine hissed behind them. "Instead, you're jumping into something else, giving up your career to be a farmer. I was just a little surprised. It's a big change for you."

"Maybe at sixty I want a big change." There was challenge in his eyes, also the familiar stubbornness.

"I guess the question is whether it's the right kind of big change. Are you sure this is what's going to make you happy?"

"I'm pretty sure I know what's not," he answered instead. "All things considered, it's not that much different than what I do now. For the past two years, I've been on the board of a venture firm that funds start-ups. This is a start-up, too, it's just more down-to-earth."

"Literally," Larkin murmured, thinking of the time she'd spent the night before digging dirt out from under her fingernails.

"I don't think that's bad. Or maybe it can be. Your hands look like you shoved them into an eggbeater," he observed. "Don't you have gloves?"

She eyed the scrapes and broken nails. Odd how they didn't appall her nearly as much as they would have a month before. "I have gloves, but some things you have to do barehanded."

"And how is it that you disapprove of me farming so strongly that you flew across the country to talk me out of it, but it's okay for you to do it yourself? Ignoring, for the moment, the question of why you're doing it," he added.

"Because I'm not investing a small fortune. I'm not walking away from my life like you are. I'm not planning on staying."

"I don't know that I'm walking away from so very much," he said broodingly. "I look at my life right now and all I can think is I've been doing what I do for way too long. And for all the people I know in Manhattan, there's not a damn one of them I would really miss. This place seems real. The people seem real. Molly seems—"

"Great, I know," Larkin finished for him. "I like her, too. But don't you think you're rushing into this a little bit?

Moving in lock, stock and barrel after knowing her, what, three weeks?"

"I haven't moved in lock, stock and barrel, and I won't be. I'm staying at a hotel in Montclair." He narrowed his eyes as she opened up a cupboard and brought out a pair of mugs. "And I suppose you're staying here."

"In the guest room." At his skeptical look, she rolled her eyes. "I'm twenty-seven, Dad. And, no, I'm not diving into something with Christopher. Not like you are with Molly."

"Molly and I are friends."

She raised her chin. "And Christopher and I are friends."

"Judging by the way you were standing together when I drove up, you have a very different definition of that than I do," he said.

Abruptly, she felt fond of him. "Not yet. But if that changes, it'll be my decision. I am an adult now."

"That happened when I wasn't looking." His voice was quiet, feistiness replaced by regret.

"There's a lot more ahead. We just took a long time-out, you and I. Look at it this way, now you get a chance to know and love me all over again." Her tone was light as she pressed a kiss on the top of his head.

It brought a smile. "You used to do that when you wanted money for clothes."

She handed him the coffee and sat. "Well, since you brought it up, there are some nice overalls in the L.L. Bean catalog," she began.

Molly was standing at her sink washing peppers when she heard the knock on the door and turned to see Carter.

"Well, look who's back," she said, wiping her hands on a dish towel.

"You should keep this door locked," he admonished her. "Anyone could come walking in."

"Like you." She leaned in to kiss his cheek. "And wouldn't that be a shame if it had been locked? Anyway, who do I need to protect myself from? Family? Friends? The squirrels?"

"You shouldn't be so trusting."

"I refuse not to be," she countered. "I've made some iced tea. Why don't you go out on the porch? I'll bring you some."

Flies ticked against the screens of the broad veranda that ran along the front of the old farmhouse. There had been a time when her sons had put up hammocks and slept out there on a hot night. Now, the hammocks had been replaced with wicker chairs, and a glider that she and Carter had whiled away more than one evening on during his last visit.

The afternoon was winding down, the air still warm but the shadows lengthening. "I think Indian summer may well be my favorite time of year," Molly mused as she walked onto the porch. "Next to spring, that is. And maybe fall."

"Nice that you're a woman who knows her own mind." Carter had bypassed the glider in favor of one of the wicker chairs, she saw.

She handed him his tea, then chose another chair nearby. "I'm a Trask. I was born knowing my own mind."

"So I've discovered." He gave her an opaque glance. "I stopped by Christopher's on my way in."

"Christopher's." She became very still. "I see."

"Larkin was there, although I suppose you knew that," he said, an edge to his voice. "We've talked a half-dozen times since I've been gone, Molly. When were you going to get around to telling me?"

She set her tea aside. "I wasn't."

"Why not?" he demanded.

"I didn't think it was my place," she replied evenly. "If Larkin had wanted you to know, she would have told you."

"So you'll keep secrets from me about my own daughter?"

She studied him. "Carter, family relationships are complicated, and yours and Larkin's is more complicated than most," she said after a pause. "It's not my place to decide what's a secret and what's not. You two have just come off a long separation. You need to learn to trust each other again."

His hands tightened on the wicker. "I need to trust you."

"You can. You can trust that I'm not going to try to stick myself in the middle where I'm not wanted and I don't belong."

"I need to be able to trust you to tell me things I need to know," he shot back.

Molly was already shaking her head. "If I'd told you she was here staying with Christopher, you'd have been in the car and on your way up as soon as we disconnected."

"So what if I had?" There was a flash of stubborn anger in his eyes. "She's got no business just moving in there with him."

"I'm not sure that she's moved in quite the way you think, not that it should matter. It really isn't my business but do you honestly think you can swagger in after five years and try to run her life? She's an adult now, Carter. You're going to have to get used to treating her like one."

He set his jaw. Molly waited. "That's what Larkin told me," he said finally.

"You've got a smart daughter. You should listen to her." Molly rubbed some condensation off her glass. "As far as you and I, I'm not sure what to say. I'm sorry that you feel I've betrayed you in some way, but if I had it to do over again, I'd do the same thing. I don't believe in stepping into family business, especially when we're just—"

"What?" His gaze was unwavering.

"Friends."

"Is that what we are?"

There was a flicker of temper in her eyes. "I thought so."

He tapped his fingers restlessly on the wicker. "When I saw Larkin, I realized a couple of things. I didn't like feeling blindsided, but I particularly didn't like feeling blindsided by you. Not that it's all that unfamiliar." He gave a short laugh. "I don't exactly have a stellar track record when it comes to the opposite sex."

"I see," Molly said. "Well, then I guess—"

"Let me finish, please. I'm bollixing this up. Feeling sucker punched by someone who means something to me, that's familiar. But the reasons you gave me just now for why you did what you did?" He shook his head. "I've never had anybody put my family and me first before… except Beth." He reached out his hand to hers. "I don't want to be just your friend anymore, Molly. I'd like to be…more than that."

For a moment, she didn't move. Then she slipped her fingers into his and they sat, quiet, not silent.

"So if you're not my friend, what are you?" Molly broke the stillness. "My gentleman caller?"

The corner of Carter's mouth twitched. "I could be."

"Well, gentleman caller." She stood. "Would you like to stay for dinner?"

Chapter Thirteen

He'd done business with partners before, Christopher thought. More than once, he'd met the father of a woman he'd been sleeping with. But he'd sure as hell never been interrupted by a business partner while he was holding the man's daughter with every intention of talking her straight into bed.

Even if he'd already made the decision not to do business with the partner.

He paced across the floor of his bedroom, his hair still wet from his shower. He hadn't wanted to take Carter's money from the beginning. He hadn't wanted to take anyone's money. To him, not succeeding on his own was an admission of failure.

To Carter, it was just an infusion of working capital.

Except the working capital was attached to the woman who currently gave Christopher technicolor dreams.

It hadn't been hard to agree on the bet with Larkin. He'd already just about made the decision to turn Carter down;

the call from Pure Foods had simply made it easier. His error had been in not telling Carter immediately.

An error he'd been made very aware of that afternoon.

A man didn't amass nearly a billion dollars without being able to crack down when necessary. And however his conversation with Larkin had gone, Carter Hayes had stalked out of the house and across the barnyard toward Christopher with the clear and obvious intent of rearranging some vital portion of his anatomy.

"What goes on between my daughter and you is your personal business, or so she informed me," Carter told him crisply. "But you're mixing your personal business with my financial business, and I don't like that a bit." He'd taken a breath to continue.

"I think if you check with your bank, you'll discover that the deposit's already been returned." Christopher had kept his voice mild. Best to deliver that information before the conversation went any further.

Carter stared at him like he was under a microscope. "Returned because you're sleeping with my daughter or returned because you're too damned stubborn to take anyone else's money?"

"I'm not sleeping with your daughter—not that it's any of your business—and you're a fine one to call anyone stubborn." Christopher found himself retorting.

Carter Hayes had thrown his head back and laughed. "I'm stubborn? Son, you could teach those bucks of yours a thing or two." The laughter had eased off to an occasional chuckle. "You know, I'm sorry I won't be doing business with you. Although I'm getting a feeling we'll have other opportunities." He'd turned to his car. "Speaking of stubbornness, I assume you turning down my money doesn't affect your offer to teach me farming, right?"

Christopher had blinked. "Uh, no."

"Good. See you tomorrow morning."

It had worked out for the best, Christopher thought now. So why the uneasiness?

I'm getting a feeling we'll have other opportunities.

He and Larkin had had unfinished business, he'd thought the day she'd shown up. Striking the bet had merely seemed like an opportunity to find out just how explosive it could be, work it out of their systems and be done with it. But now, he wondered. Was she a woman he could tire of or the drug that once tasted became an addiction?

The last thing he needed was to get hooked. On anyone.

He stood impatiently. There was a whole host of reasons to keep his distance, a host of reasons they didn't make sense for anything but the short-term. He'd been down that road before. He had enough going on with the farm that he didn't need to get in over his head with a woman like Larkin.

Maybe the smartest thing was to call off the bet. Tell Larkin he'd given back the money, send her on her way and not go to bed with her at all.

However much he ached to.

He stared at the clock. First thing in the morning, he'd talk to her. In the meantime, sleep just wasn't going to happen, but he had a perfect cure for that. Paperwork. In a small business, there was always paperwork—in this case a whole pile of it waiting for him downstairs next to his computer.

Impatiently, he dragged on his jeans and strode into the hall.

Only to collide with Larkin as she walked out of the bathroom, a pile of clothing in her arms. The clothing went flying, she spun around and he caught at her shoulders to steady her.

She was wrapped in that short, silky little robe of hers, fastened with just a sash. There weren't any buttons in sight. Bad thing to know, he thought. "Sorry," he said.

"I shouldn't have barged out like that."

She knelt to pick up her shirt. He tried valiantly to pay more attention to picking up her jeans than to the long, lovely legs she exposed. Short of closing his eyes or rendering himself blind, though, there was little he could do. As he reached for the denim, out of the corner of his eye he saw her pick up a bra, one of those that looked like she must have ordered it somewhere other than L.L. Bean.

Then he spied the scrap of black fabric and lace on the floor.

She hadn't gotten that at L.L. Bean, either.

The color of midnight, the color of sin, it was silky against his fingers. The way he imagined her skin would be. To touch it was to see her in it, to imagine sliding it down from her hips, inch by inch.

The blood began to pound in his head.

"You dropped this." He handed it to her.

And their fingers brushed together.

They rose at the same time, their hands touching, their gazes locked on each other. It was like iron filings and magnets, able to keep their distance until they got too close. One minute, he was registering the cool softness of her skin, the slipperiness of the silk, the next all he could feel was the heat of Larkin's body against his. This time, when the clothing dropped, neither cared.

Mouth to mouth, body to body, desire blazed up around them with an almost physical flame. For weeks, they'd been dancing around it—now they couldn't anymore, now the genie was out of the bottle and there was no putting it back. It wasn't about seduction; neither of them had patience for that. Instead, they demanded, devoured. Minutes before, Christopher had been certain he could turn away from this moment.

Now he knew it was impossible.

Larkin's mouth was avid and greedy against his, her abandon intoxicating. He feasted on her throat, inhaling the sweet scent of her. The vibration of her moan against his lips had him teetering on the edge of control.

Christopher could feel every dip and curve of her body beneath the silk as though she were naked. The smooth fabric slipped over her heated skin, a maddening barrier that let him feel so much, yet so far from enough. She twisted against him, urging him on, her hands skimming down his bare back to his jeans, slipping down under the waistband.

He heard her throaty laugh, a seduction in itself. "Going commando, hmm?"

And then he ran his hand up under her robe to feel her ass. "Just like you." He moved his hand around to the outside again, up over her hip, and to the soft swell of her breast. He could feel her, round, yielding, feel the hard, insistent bead of her nipple against his palm in the middle of all that softness.

It tore a groan from him. "God, I want you."

In answer, she pressed her open mouth to his, using the dance of tongue and lip to tell him all he needed to know.

He walked her backward into his bedroom, feeling the polished wood of the hall change to thick, deep carpet. Larkin stopped him before they reached the bed. Then he did what he'd been dreaming of for days and untied the sash at her waist, sliding his hands inside the flaps of the robe to part them and find her.

She was satin and strength, silk and heat. If the feel of her beneath the silk had aroused him, the feel of her bare skin really made him explode. He wanted to touch her everywhere. He needed to taste her even more. But most of all, he burned for the feel of her beneath him on the bed, wrapped around him, urgent against him as he buried himself in her and took them over together.

Even as he bent his head to kiss her, Larkin pulled away, letting the robe fall open, slipping it back so that her shoulders gleamed in the light from the hall. Her eyes were dark, drugged with passion. And then she shrugged and let the silk stream off her like water to pool the wood around her feet.

And Christopher swore his heart about stopped.

She was long and lovely, pale in the soft cast of light. It was impossible to believe that a woman so finely made could be as strong as he knew she was. It was impossible to believe that he'd waited so long to come to this place, this moment with her.

Any desire he'd ever felt in his life for a woman was mere delusion compared to this. Even the headiest moments had been nothing like the insatiable hunger that twisted in him now. She raised her arms to him, and he caught her up to carry her to the bed, pressing her back on the coverlet. With shaking hands, he stripped off his jeans and then eased onto the bed beside her.

Larkin caught her breath at the press of Christopher's naked body against hers. It seemed an almost unimaginable luxury, a feast that nearly overwhelmed her senses. And yet she wanted more. She'd felt the strength of his body before, but always covered, never bare like this so that she could run her hand over him and savor muscle and tendon, sinew and bone.

He didn't have the swollen physique of a gym rat, one who spent hours with the weight plates. His was a body forged by labor, sculpted by need. She traced her fingers over the swell of his chest, stroking the light dusting of hair there. Sliding her fingertips down his stomach, she was rewarded by the hiss of his breath, the tightening of muscles that corrugated his belly.

Then he was pressing her back to trail his tongue down

over her throat, her chest, to where the excruciatingly sensitive skin of her breasts began. The liquid caress had her gasping. His hand stroked up her thigh, slid over her hip, circling inward, making her tremble. She'd never been so aware of her body in her entire life, as though he were molding it, forming it with his touch.

And then his mouth closed over her nipple, and she flung her head back against the pillow. Wet heat, light scrape of teeth, it sent her clutching the sheets, gasping for air. And between her thighs a slow spiral of tension began to form.

"God, you're amazing," Christopher murmured against her skin as he ran his fingertips over her belly, so close to where she craved his touch. More, the thought drummed through her. She wanted more, needed more, needed it all. Needed him.

So soft, so responsive, he thought as she moved against him. He teased, tracing circles until he heard her impatience and felt his own. And finally, giving in to temptation, he shifted his fingers to that cleft at the top of her thighs, only to find her already slick and hot and ready.

The breath exploded out of him even as she cried out.

He wanted to taste her, he wanted to touch her, but the need, the need pounded through him. "I have to be in you," he managed, fighting for control.

"Hurry," Larkin whispered breathlessly, reaching for him.

Her touch nearly undid him. He poised himself over her, shuddering at the feel of her warm wetness against the tip of him, at the slide of her legs wrapping around him like velvet. Desperate, unable to hold back, he sank himself into her in a single move.

And they cried out as one.

She was wrapped around him. He was wrapped around her. He couldn't tell if the pounding came from her heart or his own, a pulse that set the rhythm of their coupling, the surge and flow of their bodies together.

They were racing together now, upward and upward still. The rhythm now was everything, the rhythm and the stroke of the hard length of him bringing that burst of good friction to her every time his muscles bunched and he drove into her, bringing her closer, ever closer. Impossible that she could hold out for even a moment longer, impossible that she could ever let it end. The sound of her own cries in her ears merged with that of Christopher's ragged breath as they drove together toward that destination that was not place but feeling, experience.

And then she tipped and tumbled over, jolting and tumbling in the wave of pleasure even as she heard his finishing groan.

Christopher stared up at the ceiling. Larkin lay draped over him, her breath feathering over his chest in sleep. He could feel the beat of her heart. The house was silent. The clock radio cast a green glow over the room in its march toward morning.

Morning, when he would have to tell her the bet was off.

He'd thought he was smart enough to avoid the danger. He'd thought that a little attraction was no big deal, that however much he was attracted, she wouldn't get to him. He hadn't reckoned on the fact that it wasn't just a little attraction, and that it was a very big deal indeed.

It seemed impossible to think that only a few hours before, he'd made plans to tell her about the bet, send her on her way, end things between them before he got in too deep. It seemed impossible that a few hours before, he hadn't realized that he was already sunk.

He'd figured he was too wary, too cynical to let his heart

get involved. But while he'd been busy guarding against it, she'd snuck in and gotten to him anyway. And how ironic was it that it wasn't the allure of sky-high heels and a bombshell dress that had done it but the clever comebacks of a feisty woman working at his side in jeans and gum boots?

He was in love with her, and he didn't know what the hell to do about it.

He stroked her back, and she sighed in her dreams, then nuzzled closer to him.

Everything had changed between them and yet nothing had. Her home was still elsewhere. She still had a life and a career that were light years from this farm, this house and the bed where they now lay. The only thing that was holding her here, with him, was the bet.

And so he lay in the dark, staring up at the ceiling, knowing that he had to tell her he'd given Carter's money back and knowing that he couldn't, not that day, maybe not the next. Or the next.

Because he knew when that happened, she would be gone.

And he didn't know how he was going to stand it.

Chapter Fourteen

Larkin had always avoided staying overnight with lovers. She never slept well with somebody else in the bed. She never liked the awkwardness of the morning. Easier, on the whole, to get dressed and bolt, to continue things a day or two later in a civilized venue like a restaurant, when she wasn't naked and vulnerable but was protected by the armor of clothing.

How was it that it felt so good to awaken under soft sheets and eiderdown, with Christopher warm behind her?

She'd wondered for a while—from the moment she'd met him, if she were honest—how it would be. Friends, she'd told Carter. "If that changes," she'd said as though she hadn't decided yet, when deep down inside she'd already known. Like some subsonic pulse that was felt, not heard, the wanting had been running through her ever since she'd arrived at the farm.

And the reality had put her most vivid imaginings to shame.

The room was just beginning to lighten around her. Outside, she heard a rooster crow. It wasn't fair, Larkin thought. She wasn't ready for the new day. For a moment, she wanted nothing more than to just lie there under the covers, savoring the feel of Christopher's arms wrapped around her, drifting in that half state between sleep and wakefulness.

The little stir of uneasiness brought her fully awake. That wasn't what it was supposed to be about. It was supposed to be about heat and friction and driving need, not about sweet comfort.

Heat and friction and driving need. That was what she had always relegated sex to in the past. As she always relegated relationships to the "somebody else's problem" file. If growing up with Carter had taught her nothing, it had taught her that lies and conflict and self-interest were the staples of most involvements, and if you went in expecting anything else, you were destined for disappointment. Maybe Carter could remain eternally optimistic, but Larkin had always made it her policy not to.

So why was she lying here in bed with Christopher, wanting more?

She felt lips press against her shoulder and jolted.

"You're not supposed to tense up when I do that," he murmured against her skin.

"I wasn't awake," she said.

"Liar," he mocked softly. He shifted so that she was on her back and bent to kiss her. "Good morning."

"Good morning."

"How did you sleep?"

"Well, thanks." *Amazingly well.* She was surprised to realize she had slept at all.

"And how did your upgrade work out?" he asked, a gleam of humor in his eyes as he traced his fingers down her throat.

Larkin blinked. "My upgrade?"

"From our guest room."

The corners of her mouth tugged up on their own. "Oh, quite satisfactory. Your staff was very attentive."

"That's our specialty," he said. "We're what you call a full-service operation. We'll even be serving breakfast downstairs later." He rolled over and pulled her on top of him. "And should we expect you tonight?" His expression was deadpan, but mischief lurked in his eyes.

And Larkin gave in to it. "Until the end of the month," she said.

"Excellent." He ran his hands down to cup her derriere. "Anything else we can do for you? Want to hear about our spa treatments? We have some very innovative massage techniques."

Larkin wriggled a little bit atop him and was rewarded by feeling him start to harden. "I'll bet you do," she breathed. "I'll just bet you do."

Heat and friction and driving need. And maybe, just maybe, a little bit of uncomplicated happiness.

The big farmhouse table in Christopher's kitchen was littered with boxes and tape, packing material and, above all, sealed packets of cheese. It was shipping day, the day the week's orders went out the door. In separate piles lay the order slips, the Styrofoam packages, the dry ice, the cheese and the corrugated cardboard cartons. It was up to Christopher and Larkin to pack it all.

"You know, I think we're going about this all wrong," Larkin said as she added cheese to a Styrofoam box.

"What do you mean?" Christopher glanced up from sealing a carton to stare at her.

Extraordinary that he could heat her blood with only a look. "Well, each one of us is going down the line."

"True." He slapped on a label and added the box to the stack.

"If we just stayed in one place and did one job each, it would go faster. You know, like an assembly line?"

"You think so?" He walked behind her to the other end of the table, stroking a hand over her derriere as he passed.

For an instant, Larkin's thoughts scattered like leaves whirling in the wind. Shaking her head, she started again. "Yes, I do. It would be more efficient."

"Doubtlessly." Picking up an order slip and grabbing a Styrofoam pack, Christopher started back toward her.

"I could put the cheese into the Styrofoam, and you could box and seal."

He stopped behind her. "Yeah?"

The back of her neck prickled with awareness. "There would be less walking back and forth." Her hands slowed. "We would get it done faster."

She could feel him leaning closer. "There's just one problem," he murmured.

"What?"

"I like the walking back and forth part." He pressed his lips to the nape of her neck.

And her knees turned to water. "This isn't helping," she scolded breathlessly.

He slipped his hands around her waist. "But it's fun." He trailed liquid kisses down the side of her neck.

She was sinking into lassitude and wanting. "We have to get this done."

"We're on the last two orders, and the UPS truck doesn't come for a while." Christopher leaned in to scrape his teeth along her jaw. "We've got time."

"Not while my father and Deke are around," she managed, but she groaned as his hands slipped up to cover her breasts. Then she heard tires outside. "That's the UPS truck."

It wasn't. It was Molly.

She got out of her truck beaming, in a pretty sky-colored blouse that brought out her eyes. "I made zucchini bread from the last of the crop," she called, holding up a basket. "I thought I'd bring you some."

Larkin's lips curved as they walked down the front steps and over to where she stood. "You know, I don't remember the last time I had homemade zucchini bread."

"If you look hard, I bet you'll find a few brownies tucked in there, too," Molly confided. "Maybe you can get to them before Christopher does."

The man in question snorted. "Good luck with that. We can wrestle for them," he suggested.

Flushing, Larkin elbowed him. "I don't think that will be necessary."

"Hey," he said.

Molly glanced between them; then her eyes brightened. "Farm life seems to suit you," she said to Larkin.

"That's what I keep telling her," Christopher put in.

There was a shout from the pasture with the kids. Larkin looked up to see Carter hurrying over, a goat or two in his wake. He wore grubby jeans, a denim shirt with the sleeves rolled up, work boots and a John Deere hat.

Molly crossed to the fence, laughing. "If your friends at the stock exchange could see you now," she said, shaking her head as he shoved the kids back so he could squeeze out.

He pulled off his gloves and tucked them in his back pocket. "If my friends on the stock market could see me now, they'd be green with jealousy. Watching you beats the heck out of watching the big board."

"Better than a rise in the price of gold?"

He caught her hands and grinned into her eyes. "You're pure gold all to yourself," he said and gave her a quick kiss.

Here it came again, Larkin thought.

Molly blushed and pushed him away. "You do talk."

"I'm glad you've noticed."

"I notice a lot," she said.

Carter glanced over at them. "Hey, Christopher, Deke and I got that fence fixed. Okay if I cut out for a couple of hours? There's something I need to check with Molly."

Christopher studied the shadows. "It's only a couple of hours to milking time, and we've got that under control. Why don't you go ahead and call it a day?"

"Great." Carter beamed. "I'll see you back at the house, Moll," he told her and headed toward his SUV.

Moll.

"I guess it wasn't UPS after all," Christopher said to Larkin.

"I guess not," she said shortly.

Something was wrong, he thought. It showed in the way she held herself, the way she walked, the tone of her voice. He'd stood by during the interchange with Carter and Molly, but mostly he'd studied Larkin, watching the tension gather in her shoulders.

Deke walked up. "Fence is done," he mumbled, shooting a hunted glance at Larkin. When it came to Deke, shyness didn't begin to cover it.

"Okay," Christopher said. "Go ahead and get the hogs and chickens fed, and get down a bale of hay for the goats, too."

Deke nodded and headed toward the pig barn.

Christopher turned his attention back to Larkin. "Just a wild guess," he said, "but is something wrong?"

She jumped as though her thoughts had been elsewhere. "What? No, not at all. Why?"

"Because you look upset. What's going on?"

"Nothing," she said. "We have to finish packing the orders."

He caught at her wrist. "There are only two more boxes, and UPS won't be here for an hour," he said. "Talk to me."

"Not with an audience," she said tersely as Deke came out of the pig barn to scatter feed for the chickens.

"Fine, we'll go here." And Christopher tugged her into the cheese cave.

The thick mortared doorway stuck out of the grassy hillside like the entrance to a tunnel. Inside, the air was cool, backed by the faint hum of the circulators. The fluorescents flickered on at their movement. Around them, wooden shelves rose to the ceiling, groaning with wheels of cheese that lay quietly ripening.

Larkin glared at him. "Don't manhandle me."

"I just wanted to talk with you in private. Deke won't bother us here. Now what's going on?"

"You wouldn't understand."

"Try me."

"You'll think I'm being silly." She turned away from him to pace. "It shouldn't bother me after all this time. It just pushes my buttons. It's vintage Carter. He meets a woman, falls for her like crazy and the next thing you know, they're married. And divorced."

It explained a lot, he thought. "Are you saying it's going to happen again with my aunt?"

"You've just seen the two of them together," she said instead. "You know he's sincere. You yourself told me that people can change, and maybe he has. I've just…"

"Just what?"

She let out a breath. "I've been through it too many times before." Christopher waited her out, and finally she began to talk.

"Until I was twelve, everything was wonderful. Carter

and my mom were crazy about each other. We were a real family, always together, always laughing. Like you guys." The wistful look in her eyes cut at him.

"What happened to your mother?"

Larkin looked at him. "She got killed," she said aridly. "A drunk driver. She died instantly."

Christopher slipped his arms around her. She tensed and then softened against him.

"It must have been hard." He pressed his lips to her hair.

"It was. Probably just as much on Carter, maybe more. But he got over it faster. Six months later, I had a new stepmother."

"Six months?" Christopher pulled back and stared at her.

Her smile held no humor. "Carter doesn't do alone well."

"He wasn't doing alone," Christopher said. "He had you."

"And he didn't know what to do with me. He figured his new wife would."

"And she didn't?"

Larkin moved away, bouncing her fist lightly on the wood of the shelves. "She'd married Carter for his money, not his twelve-year-old kid. I might've been a piece of furniture for all she noticed me. At least at first."

He studied her. "At first?"

"I found a way of getting her attention," Larkin said. "Getting both of their attention."

"Let me guess, trouble at school?"

"I wasn't location-specific."

"Whatever works," he said.

"It didn't have to for very long. Carter spent most of his time at work. Michelle wanted fancy dinner parties and to go out. By their first anniversary, they were fighting like cats and dogs. It didn't take too much longer for them to get divorced."

"How old were you?"

"Fourteen." It would work, then, she'd thought. She and Carter could go back to being the kind of family they'd been before her mother died. She'd get more of his time, more of his attention. More of what she needed.

But apparently what Carter had needed was a wife, and he hadn't wasted a lot of time finding a new one. "It wasn't quite a year later that he married the next one," Larkin continued. "Kayla. She liked horses and antiques."

"But not kids?"

"Her own." Larkin rubbed her arms in the chill of the cave. "I was the obstacle. As far she was concerned, I was a threat to their inheritance. She kept me out of the way as much as possible. I didn't buy into that, though."

"More acting out?"

"At least he knew I was there." She remembered those awful years when the only attention she'd ever gotten from Carter had been scowls and lectures and threats of punishment. Then again, it had been better than nothing at all.

"What were your brothers like?"

"Stepbrothers," she corrected. "They were Kayla's. The oldest one, Joshua, was awful. Indian burns, grinding the knuckles in my hand, about like you'd expect. John was a little better, but not much."

"How long was Carter married to her?"

"I think they lasted two years before the fighting started. Maybe three and a half years, all told. I was off in college by that time. I only knew wife number four in passing. I never even met number five."

"He didn't invite you to the wedding?"

The fact that he had had been the start of the problems. "We had a falling out around that time. Their divorce was final early this year, or so I had heard. I kind of had the impression he'd decided to chill a while instead of just going on to someone else. But then he met your aunt."

Larkin took a breath and looked up at him. "Christopher, I like Molly, do you understand that? It's not about her and Carter. I guess maybe it's more about me. Maybe it's just hard for me to watch because I just can't imagine this lasting anymore than any other. For anyone. Because they don't."

"That's kind of how I felt after my divorce," Christopher said quietly.

His divorce? The words shivered through her. How little she truly knew of him.

"How long were you married?" she asked.

He met her gaze. "Three years."

It took the wind out of her. Like Carter, Larkin thought numbly. "What happened?" It didn't matter. It was just further proof of what she already knew.

"I guess the simplest explanation is different expectations," Christopher said slowly. "We met while we were living in Manhattan and Washington. She didn't much care for life on a goat farm once we actually got around to doing it."

In the midst of her turmoil, she felt sympathy. "I'm sorry," she murmured.

"Don't be. In a way it was a relief."

The summary of three years, more, out of his life. Did she need more proof?

He drummed his fingers on the wood and looked at her. "But you know, my parents have been together for forty-two years. I don't know what the secret is, but I think—" He stopped.

"What?"

He raised a hand in silence to her. "Did you hear that?"

Larkin followed.

The afternoon sun was a surprise after the dim light of

the cheese cave. It was when they were crossing the barnyard that they heard it again.

A faint cry of distress coming from the barn.

Christopher shot her a look and took off at a dead run.
He was already inside when she skidded up to the door.
And when she stepped over the threshold she saw a sight
that had fear clutching at her throat—Christopher bent
over Deke, who lay on the ground, his leg twisted up at an
impossible angle.

Christopher threw a bunch of keys at her. "Bring my
truck around," he shouted. "Fast."

It looked worse than it was, Christopher told himself.

"Trying to…toss a bale down from the loft," Deke said
weakly. "Lost my damned balance. Leg hurts…like a…
bitch."

"Yeah, well, the next time you want attention, don't try
to get it by barn diving right before milking time," Christopher said, hooking Deke's arm around his neck and
gently levering him upright.

The thin strip of sunlight slanting over the floor widened
into a trapezoid as Larkin opened the main door of the
barn. Christopher could see his truck outside, motor running, doors open. Good girl, he thought.

Larkin ran over to duck under Deke's other arm.

"Look on the bright side," she told him as they walked.
"Now he'll realize how much work you do around here
so you can hit him up for a raise." Her tone was light, her
eyes worried.

And as they stepped out into the sunlight, Christopher
heard a snuffling noise that was, unbelievably, Deke laughing. "I doubt it…cheap bastard."

"That's *Mr.* Cheap Bastard, to you," Christopher corrected as they eased Deke into the truck.

"You're the boss," Larkin said. "We're allowed to complain, right, Deke?"

His face was white with pain, but he managed a ghost of a smile. "Right." He clasped her hand for a moment.

"I'm taking him directly to the E.R." Christopher strode quickly around to the driver's side. "It's the fastest way. You stay here, deal with UPS. Bring the herd down to the holding pen. I'll milk when I get home."

"God knows when that will be. I'll milk," she said.

He got behind the wheel. "You can't milk a hundred head alone."

"Of course I can." Her jaw set stubbornly. "I'll go slow. I've been doing it for going on three weeks. How bad can it be? You're wasting time," she added. "Get him to the hospital. We'll worry about the rest later."

Larkin took a breath as the goats milled about in the holding pen. She could do this. It wasn't a matter of milking a hundred goats; it was a matter of milking ten goats at a time, over and over again. She'd already run the sanitization cycle and changed over the tangle of pipes. Now she just had to do the hard part.

She opened the small door that let the herd into the main barn. Gilda led the charge down the entrance ramp and around the corner to the feeding grill, and that was when Larkin realized she'd made her first mistake. She'd forgotten to put out hay. She pelted around to the other side of the barn. Most of the herd was already up at the grid with their heads stuck through the slots, butting at each other irritably, each certain that the goat next to them had the food. Gilda and Mabel hadn't bothered with the grid. They were just going at it, a few other does standing around watching with interest.

"Stop it!" Larkin shouted. She snatched up an armful

of hay and jogged down the row, shaking it loose. For the does, food trumped anything else. They put down their heads and began to eat.

Disaster averted. Barely. Larkin hurried into the milking parlor to hang the feed bins on the milking stands, then staggered over with a bucket of grain to fill them. Forget measuring it out with a can, she figured. She'd pour it directly from the bucket and get done faster. So what if she spilled some; at least she got it done. Leaving the grain on the floor gave her only a small pang of conscience. Christopher wouldn't like it, but she couldn't spare time to sweep it up.

"Okay, okay, what's next," she asked herself aloud. She thought of Christopher.

Do it all in the same order.

It calmed her. She'd sanitized and switched the pipes so the milk would go to the pasteurizer. She'd brought the goats in and put up the feed bins. She'd uncapped the inflators and gotten out the cups for iodine and stripping the teats. And next was…?

Music. She snapped her fingers and crossed to the beat-up boom box. In time with her footsteps, thuds sounded as the first goats finished began to nudge at the trapdoor to get in.

No blues, not tonight. She needed calm not rock. She scanned across the dial until she found an indie channel with Sarah McLachlan. That was better. Exhaling, she turned to the trapdoors. She could do this. It would be fine. She pulled on the ropes to open them.

Gilda glowered back at her from eye level. The white goat moved to hurry into the milking parlor and stopped, looking around suspiciously.

"All right, already," Larkin said. "What's the problem?"

At the other door, Mabel stood stubbornly.

"Come on." Larkin checked the trapdoors, but they were up all the way. It didn't matter to Gilda and Mabel. Behind them, the other goats began to push and complain. Gilda swayed with the pressure, but dug her toes in.

"Dinner," Larkin tempted, shaking one of the feed bins. When that didn't work, she tried a more direct approach, reaching out to grab Gilda's collar. The doe shook her head mutinously and backed up.

Behind them on the ramp came the sounds of fighting.

"For God's sake, what do you want?" Larkin demanded. "The door is open, you've got your food, you've got your mus—"

And then she remembered. Blues and classic rock, Christopher had said. They hated classical. Or maybe they just didn't like anything that was different than what they knew.

Including Sarah McLachlan.

She whirled to the boom box and punched the button to start the CD player. Creedence Clearwater Revival filled the room and Gilda and Mabel jumped immediately onto the milking stands, followed by other goats.

Larkin started with Mabel's side, closing the trapdoor. At the sound of commotion behind her, she glanced back to see a traffic jam where Gilda had stopped in the middle, blocking the goats behind her.

"Come on, Gilda," Larkin snapped, pushing at the doe. Gilda bleated irritably and kicked out, but eventually she moved down. Larkin turned to monitor the other goats coming through the trapdoor. She heard a clunk.

And turned, mouth falling open in dismay.

Instead of moving down to the end of the milking stand, Gilda had somehow nudged open the exit gate and hopped down to the ground where she stood, energetically tucking into the spilled feed. Cursing, Larkin hurried over to grab her.

Meanwhile, the other goats kept pushing through the open trapdoor, fighting one another to get to the bins of feed. Of course, when they saw the spilled feed, they jumped down to where Larkin was wrestling Gilda and losing. Some of them stopped to eat, some slipped nimbly behind her, nudging open the door that led to the walkway area of the barn where hay still lay.

Meanwhile, the goats on Mabel's milking stand had finished with their grain and begun bleating and fighting.

How bad can it be?

Larkin was about to find out.

Christopher closed the door of his truck and walked to the side door of the nearly dark house. Even after he'd gotten Deke to the emergency room, it had taken hours for him to be treated. Compound fracture, they'd said. The hours had crawled by while they'd waited for a specialist and surgery, but finally Deke was safely tucked up in a hospital bed and Christopher was able to head for home.

Larkin was probably asleep. For his part, he'd be up until one in the morning, at least, dealing with the milking. One of the many pleasures of farming.

He stepped onto the sunporch that doubled as his summer living room and stopped. Larkin was stretched out on the couch fully clothed and fast asleep, looking like she'd tumbled there straight from the barnyard.

On the table beside her was a note:

Disaster doesn't begin to cover it, but we made it through. You may want to check to be sure that I didn't miss milking anybody. Things got kind of mixed up.

L

P.S. I want a raise.

He smiled and leaned in to press a kiss to her forehead. Her eyes opened. "Hi," she said in a rusty voice.

"Hey," he said.

She yawned into her fist. "Deke okay?"

"He's fine. They kept him at the hospital. Come on, let's go to bed."

"Gilda is the demon seed," she told him.

"I know," he said, swinging her up into his arms. "You can tell me all about it tomorrow."

"I smell like goat." She snuggled against his chest.

He kissed her hair. "You're perfect."

Chapter Fifteen

"They were jumping up on the hay bales?" Christopher asked, walking over to the table.

She sat in her robe, her hair spilling pale and silky over her shoulders. Glancing at the plate he carried, her eyes warmed with laughter. "Curbside service. Fancy."

"It's the least I can do." He'd let her sleep that morning, handling the milking himself, then coming in to wake her.

"Well, they weren't just jumping up and down on the hay. Gilda climbed up on the tractor seat, and I'm positive she was trying to start it up. I swear, that goat is evil."

"She's not evil. She's just misunderstood."

"Oh, I understand her all right," Larkin said darkly.

Christopher looked at her with amusement. "You sound like you're ready to go out into the field and take her on, *mano a* hoof."

She bit into a piece of bacon. "You won't want to put your money on Gilda, that's all I have to say."

"Are you kidding? After what you did last night, my money's on you."

"I kept telling myself it couldn't get any worse, but after a certain point I just figured I was bloody well going to do it. And that was about when they all started to cooperate."

"It was that steely eyed determination on your face."

She snorted. "It was the homicidal rage, more like."

"We had a full moon last night. The herd always gets a little weird. I should have thought to warn you, but I didn't figure you were actually going to try milking on your own. It's a big job for me, even."

"Ignorance can be a wonderful thing," she told him.

He leaned in and kissed her. "You are truly amazing."

"I'm glad you realized."

He'd realized. He'd realized long since. He had to come clean, Christopher thought, standing to pour coffee. Come clean, let her know what she meant to him.

And beg her to stay, if that was what it took.

"You're pathetic," he muttered to himself.

"What?" Larkin called.

"Nothing. Anyway, thanks for all of it. I drove up thinking I'd be up until at least midnight, milking. That note was the best news I'd had in years."

She took the fresh coffee. "I figured it would give me something to hold over your head."

She'd been through a trial by fire. And despite all the problems, despite everything going wrong that could go wrong, she'd finished. It was humbling. Had he called her a princess once? She was anything but.

He started in on his eggs. "You know, it occurs to me that you've been working nonstop since you got here."

"Trust me, it hasn't escaped my notice. But I figure if I'm going to win this bet, I'm going to earn it."

The bet. "Look, it's Sunday. I'm going to go see Deke, if you want to go, but otherwise, why don't you take the day off and maybe we can go grab dinner after?"

She tilted her head at him. "What, like a date?"

"Sure. If you want to."

"Just don't expect me to put out."

"I won't." He grinned. They'd go out, relax, have a bottle of wine. And when they got home, he'd tell her. "So what are you going to do with your big day off?"

"It's been so long since I've had one, I'm not sure I know. Shopping, maybe, now that I've got a date. Part of the day, anyway. I'm not going to leave you to manage things alone."

"I can handle it."

"You won't have Carter to help," she reminded him.

He shrugged. "I won't need him for what I'm doing."

Her eyes brightened. "What's that?"

"Nothing special," he said. "I'll probably take the goats for a walk."

She stared. "You what?"

"Take them for a walk."

She folded her arms. "I'm definitely coming back. This I gotta see."

"So why do you walk your goats, Dr. Doolittle?"

They stood by a pasture where Christopher had just let out a couple dozen does. They clearly knew what was coming, clustering around him, tails flipping in excitement.

Except for Tallulah, who made a beeline for Larkin.

"Traitor," he told Tallulah.

"She's got good taste," Larkin defended, rubbing Tallulah's neck while the little goat chuckled deep in her throat.

He leaned in for a quick kiss that stretched into something longer. "They like it," he said when he'd finished, even as her head was still spinning. "They're not really made to eat grass. They're supposed to eat bushes and twigs and bark." He started toward the woods beyond the far pasture, the goats clustered around him like some animal fan club.

"Twigs and bark? So we're going out on the goat equivalent of a picnic?"

His smile flashed. "If you like."

The contrast was remarkable. When they were coming into the barn, the goats always ran full tilt. Once they were loose, Larkin would've expected them to make a break for it. Instead, they stayed near Christopher, dashing off a few steps to investigate a particularly tempting patch of grass, but keeping an eye on him as he passed and always running to catch up before he got too far away.

Midday sun slanted through the leaves overhead as the group crossed into the woods, following a pine needle–covered path apparently well familiar to the goats. Some stopped at every bush; others ran ahead to what were apparently favorites, taking a judicious mouthful here, tearing off a full branch there.

Tallulah held out for the maple saplings, nibbling at branches with gusto.

"You know, I think today at the hospital was the first time Deke's ever made eye contact with me," Larkin said thoughtfully.

Christopher nodded. "I'm still kind of amazed. I mean, usually it takes a year or two for Deke to even speak to someone, let alone look at them." He caught her hand in his. "I'd say you charmed him. I know you charmed me."

She couldn't entirely suppress the little burst of pleasure. She'd gotten so used to them, his little flashes of sweetness. She couldn't imagine what it would be like when she was gone. But then she remembered how he'd talked about his marriage. A relief, he'd said, talking about the end.

And their end was in sight. She wasn't going to think about it. She wasn't going to think about the fact that in less than two weeks, she'd be gone.

Instead, she watched Tallulah scalp a maple. "I think you're going to be down a tree there."

"It's good. I need to thin them out."

"So this is all your property?" she asked.

"About sixty acres, all told. I started out with eighteen, but I've been adding on whenever I get a chance."

"So how far does it run? Show me a landmark."

"From here?" He shrugged. "As far as you can see."

"Seriously?"

"Seriously." He reached out and snared her hand.

Cicadas buzzed overhead as they strolled along the sun-dappled path through the woods. His woods, Larkin thought, feeling something stir inside her. There was some-thing about a man walking on land that he owned, a pride that was somehow both alluring and endearing.

"I can see why you love it." The words were out before she knew she was going to say them.

Christopher stopped and stared at her. "What?"

"This." She waved a hand, encompassing the woods, the herd, the farm all at once. "I get it. I understand why it matters to you. I can see why you'd never want to leave."

"Don't tell me farming has gotten to you at last." There was humor in his voice—and a hint of something else just underneath.

Nerves billowed up. She'd said too much. "Don't laugh at me," she muttered, walking away. "You know, Tallulah, you try to say something nice…"

He took two swift steps, turning her and catching her face in his hands to press his lips to hers.

It wasn't about heat. It wasn't about sweetness. There was some special intensity to it, as though there was no her and no him, just the two of them flowing together. Time became plastic, immaterial.

And then Christopher broke the kiss and stared down at her. "I need to tell you something."

The tension in his voice, the tautness to his expression made her instantly uneasy. "You need to tell me something? I'm not sure I like the sound of that."

"It's not bad, once you understand it."

Which had to mean it was very bad, indeed. Larkin studied him closely. "Okay, go ahead."

He exhaled. "I gave Carter his money back."

It was the last thing she expected to hear. She stared at him with narrowed eyes. "You what?"

"I gave Carter his money back."

And it was as though everything inside her stopped.

It was done. She should have felt relief. She'd gotten what she wanted without even having to work through the month. The bet was over, she realized in a rush. Which carried a corollary: it was time to leave.

No. The reaction was visceral and sudden, shocking her in its intensity. And in a flash, she knew. She was supposed to be eager to walk away, to get back to her life. Instead, she'd let herself get caught up in the farm, caught up in the work. Caught up in Christopher. She, who'd spent a lifetime avoiding needing another. She, who knew what always happened in the end. She, who knew better than anyone how badly it could hurt to fall when there was no net below. And yet she'd let herself get involved.

And she had no idea what happened now.

Anxiety clutched her throat. "You gave it back?" She licked her lips. "When?"

His eyes flicked to the side.

Suddenly she felt cold all over. Knots formed in her stomach. "When did you give it back, Christopher?" she asked, her voice colored by the chill inside her.

"Before I tell you, I want you to give me a chance to explain," he said.

The worst words to hear. "I don't want an explanation," she said as levelly as she could. It was happening already, the inevitable lies, the betrayals. What she'd always known happened when you opened yourself up to another. "I want to know when you gave Carter his money back. Or when the bet was officially off. After all, if you've already made good on the payoff, there really is no point in continuing a bet, is there? At least no honest point to it."

"But that's just it. To me, the bet wasn't about Carter's money—"

"Of course it was," she snapped. "That's all it was about, doing whatever it took to get your hooks out of Carter."

Temper flared in his eyes. "I never wanted your father's money. I didn't ask for it, and I was sorry I let him talk me into it almost as soon as it happened."

"Oh, sure," she said scathingly. "He just twisted your arm and said, 'Take my money or else.'"

"He showed up here with Molly all hot to buy a place and play *Green Acres.* I was trying to keep him from taking a bath."

"And you agreed to take his money in order to prevent him from wasting it on someone else's farm. What a guy."

"No, I agreed to let him work here until he learned what the hell he was doing so that if he wound up sinking a million or two into a place, he'd last longer than a couple of weeks," Christopher retorted. "The only problem is that

I'm in the process of going broke. He offered the money because he wanted to keep the farm operating long enough that he could learn what he needed to know. And I didn't see a problem with it because I figured that if he quit after a week and a half, I could just give him the money back.

"But then you showed up trash-talking so, yeah, the bet seemed like a pretty good idea, because I never figured you'd make good on it either. Except this whole thing has turned out a lot different than I expected."

"Boy, is that an understatement." She stalked away and rounded on him. "All of which is beside the point."

"It's exactly the point," he returned.

"It's a simple question, Christopher. When did you give my father's money back?"

"But it's—"

"When?"

He locked eyes with her. "Two weeks ago."

It took her breath. "Two weeks?" she repeated when she found her voice. "Two *weeks*? You let me work fourteen and fifteen hours a day, knowing that the only reason I was doing it was to get you to do something you'd already done?" Her voice rose. "Did you think you were doing me a favor letting me work here? Did you think I was having fun?" It was easier, so much easier, to strike out than to feel, easier to focus on the anger than the hurt.

He whitened. "What was all that about just a little while ago, the whole 'I get it' thing? Was that just a good-sounding line? I thought we were doing something here."

She wasn't going to think about it. He'd lied to her. She'd let herself fall for him and it was already going just the way she'd always feared. "Sure we were doing something. You were lying and I was providing slave labor."

"This wasn't about getting slave labor—"

"Then what was it?" she demanded, striding up to him.

"Company in the cheese room? A chaperone for the goats? Entertain—" She stopped. "No."

"No what?"

"Oh, no. You bastard," she said venomously. "This whole thing was about sleeping with me, wasn't it? To extend the bet because you wanted me in your bed."

"It wasn't about sleeping with you."

"I'll say. We didn't do a whole lot of sleeping." She struck out to hurt. She'd let him matter. She'd let him get under her guard and now she was the one who felt cut open.

"Dammit, Larkin, it wasn't about the sex," he shouted. "Will you stop for a minute and let me talk? You want to know why I didn't tell you? I didn't tell you because I knew as soon as I did, there'd be no reason for you to stay. And I just wanted a little more time before you left."

He took a breath and stared at her. "I wanted that time because I was falling in love with you."

And in that moment she hated him because of the instant joy and hope that swept over her before the anger came rolling back. Because he'd made her vulnerable. Because he'd lied. Because he'd stood the day before and told her, "It was a relief…" in talking about the end of a marriage.

Because he'd made her love him.

Unable to keep still, she stalked away, then whirled back to him. "What is it that makes people think that 'I love you' is a fix-it for a lie?"

"Larkin—"

"It doesn't make it all better, Christopher." She cut him off. "It's not some magic spell. Do you forget what I grew up with? This is always how it starts—arguments and lies, with a little Band-Aid of 'I love you' to patch things over. And the next time the cut goes a little deeper and the Band-Aid doesn't work so well. And the next time it's even worse.

"You sit here and tell me you love me when the whole

time you were keeping things from me." *And making me fall in love with you.* "And the next time, it'll be the excuse for something else until anything we might have had is gone and you're relieved to have it over. Well, I'm not sticking around for that."

. Behind her, a ruckus broke out as Gilda and Mabel squared off together. Christopher glanced over, then fastened his gaze on Larkin. "Don't walk away from this."

"There is no this," she threw back.

"We're not done with this conversation."

Larkin looked at the fight, listening to the bleats of the goats watching. "Tell it to the does. They're girls. Maybe they'll fall for it."

And she turned and walked away.

By the time he got back to the house, she was already out in the yard, back in the clothing she'd arrived with, carrying a plastic grocery bag and nothing else.

Christopher felt the clutch of apprehension.

"Where are you going?" he asked, stopping in front of her car.

Larkin looked down at the bag she held. Her face was pale, her eyes unnaturally bright. "The bet's over and I'm gone. Wasn't that what we said?"

It was like being sucker punched. He'd known she was going to go.

He'd never thought about actually watching her leave.

"We said a lot of stuff. Look, I know you're ticked off and hurt and upset, but don't walk away from this. Let's talk about it."

"I don't want to hear what you have to say. Time for you to find someone else to play with."

He knew the bright, careless tone was intended to hurt. That didn't stop it from getting to him. "Playing? Is that what it was when we were in bed together?" Even he could hear the edge in his voice.

"Stop it." She went to brush past him.

"I mean it. You can be pissed off and hurt and frustrated and betrayed all you like, but don't sit there and tell me that what we had was the usual stuff." He took a step closer to her. "Do you remember what it was like that first night?" he demanded. "Do you?"

"It wasn't real," she cried out passionately.

"It was," he countered. "That was it—that was when I figured out how I felt about you."

"You mean while you were lying to me?" she flung out.

And suddenly he understood. "This isn't about the lie at all, is it?" he said slowly. "It's about you being scared of being involved with anyone. It's about you being scared of opening yourself up to anything real."

"There isn't anything real. Things don't last—you said it yourself yesterday."

"They do last."

"You want to talk about real? How do you get married and live with someone for three years and then say no big deal when it's over? How do you talk about a marriage like it was nothing at all?"

"Because it wasn't right. Because we didn't connect." He took a breath. "Because I never, ever felt about her the way I feel about you."

The words rang in the silence. Larkin moved her head as though to ward them off. "Words," she said. "It's how you act that counts. You can't just create some alternate reality to make people do what you want. You can't say you care about someone and then lie to them."

Abruptly all the anger went out of him. "Because I thought it was the only way I could keep you here," he said quietly. "And it looks like I was right."

Chapter Sixteen

Escape. It was the only thing she could let herself think about. So she got in the car and drove. She concentrated on the curves, passing the other vehicles, following the right highways. If she concentrated on driving, if she focused hard enough on the calls, she wouldn't have to think.

And if she didn't think, she wouldn't be conscious of this feeling that her heart was a crystal bubble set to shatter at any moment. She wouldn't remember Christopher's face, his words.

And she wouldn't remember how it felt when she'd driven away.

She made it as far as the airport in Boston before she thought to call Carter.

"Larkin," he answered, "how are you?"

How was she? There were no words for how she was.

Heartbreak alone would have been too easy. Instead, it was a mix of anger, betrayal, longing and loss, all inextricably bound.

"I'm fine," she sighed in answer. "How are you?"

"Great."

"I just wanted to let you know that I'm at the airport. I'm going home."

"Has there been some kind of an emergency?" he asked instantly.

"No," she said.

"But what about Christopher? He just lost Deke. You can't leave him without help."

"You'll be there. He managed when it was just him and Deke. I expect he can manage with just him and you."

"Are you all right?"

"Of course I am. I'm just tired."

He was silent for a long moment. "I'm sorry you have to go. When are you coming back out?"

It broke her heart. "Dad, I'm not. I'm done with the farm."

And done with Christopher.

She wasn't sure she could stand it. "Are you there?" she asked.

"Sure. I guess I'm just a little surprised that you're leaving. I thought things were working pretty well with you and Christopher. And I'm sorry I'm not going to be seeing you all the time anymore. I'd kind of gotten to like that."

"I'd kind of gotten to like that, too," she said. "Maybe when I get back you could come visit me."

"Get back from where?"

"Paris, for starters. Maybe Amsterdam, Mikonos. I need a change of scenery."

"That sounds less like you're running to something and more like you're running away."

She didn't have an answer. "I've got to go. I'm here in the terminal. You've got my number, so stay in touch."

"You've got my number, too."

"Yes."

"I expect you to use it."

Christopher stood by the feed truck, watching the grain pour into his storage silo. He turned to the driver with a frown. "That's not right. I have a ton coming, Gene."

Gene looked down. "Sorry, this is what they told me to bring."

Christopher studied him. "You can tell me the truth, Gene," he said quietly.

Gene adjusted his ball cap. "Your credit's no good, Chris. I got you as much as I could. I'm sorry."

"Don't be," Christopher said. "I knew this was coming."

"I feel like hell about it."

"It'll be okay," Christopher said and watched him get back into the cab of his truck.

Christopher blew out a breath. So it had come to this. What kind of idiot was he that he'd had the money in his hands and he'd been too stubborn to take it? And how much worse was it that deep down, he knew the reason he hadn't wanted to take it from the beginning was in part because of Larkin? Larkin, who had changed everything. Larkin, who had made his life complete.

Larkin, who had walked away.

He walked across the barnyard and over to one of the pastures with the does. Most of the herd was up the hill. When he approached the fence, he saw a shape detach itself and come running down the hill toward him, tail flipping, bleating. It was Tallulah.

She came to a stop in front of the fence and looked up at him, perplexed. She gave a quizzical bleat.

"No," he told her, "she's not here."

She bleated again.

"I'm sorry if you don't believe it, but that's the way it is. You'd better get used to it."

He wished he could take his own advice. Einstein had been right. Everything was relative, especially time. Larkin had been on the farm two and a half weeks. She'd been gone almost three, and he still missed her as much as he had the day she walked out. Larkin had been the smart one—she'd left. He'd stayed, and everywhere he looked he saw reminders of her absence, things they had done together, things they had built.

It was the same as when Nicole had left, and yet it wasn't at all. By the time Nicole had walked out, the two of them had burned away any feeling they'd had for each other. Even at its brightest, it had never come close to what he'd felt with Larkin.

And the hell of it was, no matter how hard he tried, he couldn't burn out the feeling for Larkin. He still loved her as much as he had the day she'd left.

In his pocket, his phone rang. He pulled it out.

"Christopher? Dale White over at Pure Foods. Are you near your office?"

"I'm outside, why?"

"You take a look at your fax machine. Your first order's waiting."

The first order. The lifeline he needed. He should have felt relief, but it was swamped by something else.

He'd never been one for regret, figuring that it was a waste of time, that he couldn't change the past, only the future. There was no point in regret, but it was regret he felt now.

If it had only happened earlier. If it had happened four weeks before, everything would have been perfect. But it was foolish to think that. The problem wasn't the money. The problem had never been the money. The problem was Larkin, and until she could get past her own demons, there was never going to be any hope for them.

Tallulah gave him a last disappointed look and turned to trudge back up the hill.

I'm sorry if you don't believe it, but that's the way it is. You'd better get used to it.

And he needed to get used to it, too.

In the end, Larkin went back to L.A. As much as part of her wanted to escape, it felt too much like running. But it all felt pointless—the endless rounds of clubs, Pilates, restaurant dinners. She pushed her agent to get her as much work as possible, but standing around backstage at fashion shows while the models around her chittered like brightly plumaged birds only left her feeling bored and useless.

She missed working hard. She missed dropping into bed at the end of the day totally exhausted but knowing that she'd gotten things done. She missed watching the silly behavior of the kids. She missed Tallulah.

And most of all, she missed Christopher.

The ache was the first thing she felt in the morning and the last thing she thought about as she fell asleep at night. It was a constant companion of her days. She'd get over it, she told herself.

She wished she could believe it. And for a moment, just a moment, she gave in to it and let her head fall in her hands. She just had to get through this moment, and the next moment, and the next after that. And someday, she wouldn't be surviving her days one second at a time.

She heard the *Lost* ring tone of her BlackBerry. It was Carter.

"Hey, kiddo, how are you?" he said.

Larkin gathered herself. "I'm okay, how about you?" she asked, doing her best to inject some brightness into the words.

"I'm in L.A.," he said. "Why don't you come have a late lunch with your old man?"

For the first time since she'd left Vermont, she gave a genuine smile. "You're here in town? That's great. Give me a half hour and I'll be there."

It was a chophouse, Carter's favorite type of restaurant. The booths were black leather with exposed brass nail-heads, the martinis were icy, the steaks were thick. She kissed his cheek and sat down across from him.

"What brings you here? Are you back to being the globetrotting business magnate?"

He gave a broad smile. "Not exactly. Still working on the farm with Christopher. He got a big new contract with a grocery chain, and he's trying to ramp up. He needs all the help he can get."

"It's good he's got you," she said.

"Well, he's not going to have me much longer. Things are changing." His eyes glimmered with excitement.

And Larkin's heart sank. She knew that look.

Carter took a swallow of his drink and folded his hands. "Molly and I are getting married."

She didn't answer right away. Instead, she adjusted her cutlery.

Carter watched her. "I take it you don't approve."

"I think Molly's great. I just…I guess I was hoping that this time around you'd give it some time. Get to know her."

"I do know her," he said.

"Dad, you met her two months ago. How can you possibly know her?" She hadn't known Christopher; she hadn't known Christopher at all.

"It's right, Larkin." There was quiet certainty in his voice, but she'd heard it all before.

"If it's right, why not give it time? It'll still be right next summer. It'll still be right the summer after that. I mean, you've only been divorced since January. Couldn't you just let a year go by before you recite marriage vows again?"

The stubborn look glimmered in his eyes. "Maybe I don't want to."

And abruptly the frustration hit. "I don't understand you. You marry and it doesn't work. You marry and it doesn't work. How can you trust yourself?" And how could she ever trust herself? "Every time you think this is the one. Every time you turn out to be wrong and you just wind up getting run through the mill again."

"Thanks for the reminder," he said, an edge to his voice.

"I'm not trying to give you a hard time, but I just don't understand. It hasn't worked for you four times in a row. I don't see how you keep coming back to it again and again."

"And I don't see how you've never done it once," he shot back. "I don't mean fooling around with a guy. I mean signing on for the long-term."

"Oh, like you did with Celine and Michelle and Kayla?" she snapped, rising to her feet.

"Like I did with your mother."

The sudden silence between them was deafening amid the quiet of the restaurant's midafternoon lull.

Carter let out a long breath. "I've made mistakes, Larkin. I've always gone looking for what I had with your mother because once you have that—" he swallowed "—it's pretty damned tough to do without. I don't blame myself for trying with the marriages. But what I do blame myself for is that the fallout left you so scared of anything to do with a long-term tie that you won't even try."

"That's not true," she said in a low voice, even as she knew it was.

"I used to tell myself that you were just too young. I'd hoped that maybe during the time we were apart, you'd found someone. And then when you met Christopher, after I saw you together on the farm, working…" He exhaled. "You know how I made my money?"

Larkin blinked at the sudden shift. "What do you mean? Futures trading, right?"

"By playing the market. By taking risks. You can't predict the future. There aren't any guarantees. What you do is look at the big picture and decide whether you want to take a risk. I'm ready to take a risk with Molly. I'm just sorry that you weren't willing to do that with Christopher."

She'd been here before with him—a conversation that started out talking about Carter and yet another marriage and suddenly turned into a discussion of her personal life. "What do you know about Christopher and me?"

"I know he agreed to take three quarters of a million from me for his farm. And then you showed up and he gave it back. That tells me all I need to know right there. It wasn't that he didn't need the money. It was that he didn't want the money tied with you. And he went with what was most important to him. He went with you."

"He lied to me."

"He got too close to you. He put everything he had out there and scared the hell out of you."

"That's not—" True, was what she'd started to say, but the word died in her throat.

And suddenly she knew. She shook her head slowly. "I've been a fool, haven't I?"

"You didn't invent it—plenty of people have before. The thing is admitting it."

"You're right." She rose. "I'm sorry, I can't finish lunch with you."

Carter grinned. "That's okay, we'll finish this up when we're back in Vermont."

Christopher stood on the path in the woods, the goats around him chewing busily, tearing at the underbrush. The wind rattled the trees. The colors were changing, the thick carpet of leaves underfoot. He blessed the seasonal change because it made it look different than it had when he'd been there with Larkin. He blessed the change because it made it hurt a little less.

Tallulah walked up to him and touched her head against his knee. "Still not here, kiddo," he said.

Tallulah went straight off to take a bite off a maple sapling, then wandered back over with a wistful bleat.

Christopher knelt down to scratch her ears. "I don't know what to tell you. You're just going to have to deal with her being gone."

"Or maybe she'll get her head on straight and show up on her own," a voice said behind him.

And he turned to see Larkin standing there. She wore jeans and a T-shirt, her hair down loose. She looked very young. She held the twig that she twisted in her hand even as Tallulah ran over to her.

"You know, I thought it was strange when we took the goats for a walk that they stayed right by you instead of running away," she said. "But I guess maybe I can understand. They know that there are predators out there. They've been trained to be wary their whole lives. And sometimes when that happens, it's hard to change the way you act."

Christopher straightened slowly.

Larkin swallowed. "You asked me once to let you explain. I need you to let me explain now."

"All right," he said.

"You were right that day—I am scared. I spent a lifetime watching all the worst things happen in every relationship around me. I guess like the goats, I always figured that bad stuff was out there waiting. That's why they stay around you. Because you make them feel safe." She blinked rapidly. "The morning after we first got together, I woke up thinking that I just felt safe there with you."

He could feel each individual beat of his heart. He didn't dare speak.

She moistened her lips. "I want that. I want to try with you. I want to live here on the farm. I want that more than anything. And I know I screwed up." She rushed on. "I got scared. I probably will again. But I want this, Christopher. I want it so much. Just please tell me you'll give it a try."

He reached out and caught her to him. "That's all I ever wanted, to give it a try."

She moistened her lips. "Remember how I told you I understand why you love this life? And you asked me later if those were just words?" She shook her head. "It's not. I do get it. I didn't at first, but I love this life. I love what you do here." She swallowed. "I love you."

The words hung in the air. He couldn't get a breath.

Larkin blinked quietly. "Say something," she whispered.

Instead, he whirled her around, pressing his mouth to hers. "Say it again," he demanded.

Larkin's lips twitched. "I love you."

"Again."

"I love you."

He pressed his mouth to hers. "I'm nuts about you. You can't possibly imagine how much. I've been going crazy here."

"I'm sorry, for all of it. Sometimes it takes me a while."
He squeezed her. "You're worth waiting for."

"You're worth waiting for." She ran her fingers up through his hair. "And I'm going to spend every single day doing my best to make you happy."

"No more than I will. You can't possibly imagine how great we're going to be together."

She grinned at him. "Want to bet?"

Epilogue

It was a symphony in white, as all the best weddings were. White roses, white satin ribbons, white tulle swagged above the windows of the Hotel Mount Jefferson's conservatory. Even the scene beyond the semicircular wall of glass was white, the mountains covered in a thick layer of snow against the vivid blue sky, as though to celebrate the day.

Molly blinked. "Look at me, crying."

"Isn't that what women do at weddings?" Carter asked, pulling a snowy linen handkerchief out of his pocket.

"It was just such a gorgeous wedding," she said to Larkin, who stood by in a beautifully cut column of white satin. Molly took her hand. "You looked so beautiful."

"That's what I told her," Christopher said. "Didn't I, Mrs. Trask?" He leaned in to kiss his wife.

Larkin giggled. "Oh, gosh, I am Mrs. Trask, aren't I?"

"You are, and you're going to stay that way for the duration, if I have anything to say about it."

Larkin reached out for Molly's hand. "I thought your wedding was lovely, too."

Molly glanced down at the white suit she wore. "You didn't think the red roses in the bouquet were too much?"

Larkin smiled, "Not unless you felt they were too much in mine," she answered, holding up her own matching bouquet. "But what do you want? It's Valentine's Day."

"I told Carter the only reason he wanted to get married on Valentine's Day was so that he wouldn't forget our anniversary," Molly said.

"Are you kidding?" Carter asked. "It'll make it harder than ever to remember."

"Why's that?" she asked.

He leaned down to kiss her. "Because every day's Valentine's Day with you."

Christopher and Larkin walked to the windows arm in arm and looked out over the mountains.

"I love you so much." Larkin turned to him. "You know, sometimes you have those moments that you look at your life and you just say, 'wow'?" He nodded. "Wow," she whispered.

"Wow, indeed," he said and pressed a kiss on her.

CELEBRATE
60 YEARS
OF PURE READING PLEASURE
WITH HARLEQUIN®!

**We'll be spotlighting a different series
every month throughout 2009
to celebrate our 60th anniversary.**

Look for Harlequin® Blaze™ in March!

O-60

*After all, a lot can happen in 60 years,
or 60 minutes...or 60 seconds!*

Find out what's going down in Blaze's
hcart-stopping new miniseries *0-60!*
Getting from "Hello" to "How was it?"
can happen fast....

*Look for the brand-new **0-60** miniseries in March 2009!*

www.eHarlequin.com   HBRIDE09

HARLEQUIN® Romance®

This February the Harlequin® Romance series will feature six Diamond Brides stories featuring diamond proposals and gorgeous grooms.

Share your dream wedding proposal and you could WIN!

The most romantic entry will win a diamond necklace and will inspire a proposal in one of our upcoming Diamond Grooms books in 2010.

In 100 words or less, tell us the most romantic way that you dream of being proposed to.

For more information, and to enter the Diamond Brides Proposal contest, please visit
www.DiamondBridesProposal.com

Or mail your entry to us at:

IN THE U.S.: 3010 Walden Ave., P.O. Box 9069, Buffalo, NY 14269-9069
IN CANADA: 225 Duncan Mill Road, Don Mills, ON M3B 3K9

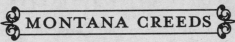

REQUEST YOUR FREE BOOKS!
2 FREE NOVELS PLUS 2 FREE GIFTS!

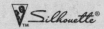

SPECIAL EDITION®
Life, Love and Family!

YES! Please send me 2 FREE Silhouette Special Edition® novels and my 2 FREE gifts (gifts are worth about $10). After receiving them, if I don't wish to receive any more books, I can return the shipping statement marked "cancel." If I don't cancel, I will receive 6 brand-new novels every month and be billed just $4.24 per book in the U.S. or $4.99 per book in Canada, plus 25¢ shipping and handling per book and applicable taxes, if any*. That's a savings of at least 15% off the cover price! I understand that accepting the 2 free books and gifts places me under no obligation to buy anything. I can always return a shipment and cancel at any time. Even if I never buy another book from Silhouette, the two free books and gifts are mine to keep forever.

235 SDN EEYU   335 SDN EEY6

Name	(PLEASE PRINT)
Address	Apt. #
City	State/Prov.	Zip/Postal Code

Signature (if under 18, a parent or guardian must sign)

Mail to the **Silhouette Reader Service:**
IN U.S.A.: P.O. Box 1867, Buffalo, NY 14240-1867
IN CANADA: P.O. Box 609, Fort Erie, Ontario L2A 5X3

Not valid to current subscribers of Silhouette Special Edition books.

Want to try two free books from another line?
Call 1-800-873-8635 or visit www.morefreebooks.com.

* Terms and prices subject to change without notice. N.Y. residents add applicable sales tax. Canadian residents will be charged applicable provincial taxes and GST. Offer not valid in Quebec. This offer is limited to one order per household. All orders subject to approval. Credit or debit balances in a customer's account(s) may be offset by any other outstanding balance owed by or to the customer. Please allow 4 to 6 weeks for delivery. Offer available while quantities last.

Your Privacy: Silhouette is committed to protecting your privacy. Our Privacy Policy is available online at www.eHarlequin.com or upon request from the Reader Service. From time to time we make our lists of customers available to reputable third parties who may have a product or service of interest to you. If you would prefer we not share your name and address, please check here. ☐

Harlequin® Historical
Historical Romantic Adventure!

The Aikenhead Honours

HIS CAVALRY LADY
Joanna Maitland

Dominic Aikenhead, spy against the Russians, takes a young soldier under his wing. "Alex" is actually Alexandra, a cavalry maiden who also has been tasked to spy on the Russians. When Alexandra unveils herself as a lady, will Dominic flee, or embrace the woman he has come to love?

Available March 2009
wherever books are sold.

The Inside Romance newsletter has a NEW look for the new year!

Same great content, brand-new look!

The Inside Romance newsletter is a FREE quarterly newsletter highlighting our upcoming series releases and promotions!

Click on the Inside Romance link on the front page of **www.eHarlequin.com** or e-mail us at insideromance@harlequin.ca to sign up to receive your FREE newsletter today!

You can also subscribe by writing to us at: HARLEQUIN BOOKS Attention: Customer Service Department P.O. Box 9057, Buffalo, NY 14269-9057

Please allow 4-6 weeks for delivery of the first issue by mail.

You're invited to join our Tell Harlequin Reader Panel!

By joining our new reader panel you will:

- Receive Harlequin® books—they are FREE and yours to keep with no obligation to purchase anything!
- Participate in fun online surveys
- Exchange opinions and ideas with women just like you
- Have a say in our new book ideas and help us publish the best in women's fiction

In addition, you will have a chance to win great prizes and receive special gifts! See Web site for details. Some conditions apply. Space is limited.

To join, visit us at
www.TellHarlequin.com.

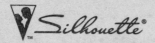

COMING NEXT MONTH
Available February 24, 2009

#1957 TRIPLE TROUBLE—Lois Faye Dyer
Fortunes of Texas: Return to Red Rock

Financial analyst Nick Fortune was a whiz at numbers, not diapers. So after tragedy forced him to assume guardianship of triplets, he was clueless—until confident Charlene London became their nanny. That's when Nick fell for Charlene, and the trouble really began!

#1958 TRAVIS'S APPEAL—Marie Ferrarella
Kate's Boys

Shana O'Reilly couldn't deny it—family lawyer Travis Marlowe had some kind of appeal. But as Travis handled her father's tricky estate planning, he discovered things weren't what they seemed in the O'Reilly clan. Would an explosive secret leave Travis and Shana's budding relationship in tatters?

#1959 A TEXAN ON HER DOORSTEP—Stella Bagwell
Famous Families

More Famous Families from Special Edition! Abandoned by his mother, shafted by his party-girl ex-wife, cynical Texas lawman Mac McCleod was over love. Until a chance reunion with his mother in a hospital, and a choice introduction to her intriguing doctor, Ileana Murdock, changed everything....

#1960 MARRYING THE VIRGIN NANNY—Teresa Southwick
The Nanny Network

Billionaire Jason Garrett would pay a premium to the Nanny Network for a caregiver for his infant son, Brady. And luckily, sweet, innocent nanny Maggie Shepherd instantly bonded with father and son, giving Jason a priceless new lease on love.

#1961 LULLABY FOR TWO—Karen Rose Smith
The Baby Experts

When Vince Rossi assumed custody of his friend's baby son after an accident, the little boy was hurt, and if it weren't for Dr. Tessa McGuire, Vince wouldn't know which end was up. Sure, Tessa was Vince's ex-wife and they had a rocky history, but as they bonded over the boy, could it be they had a future—together—too?

#1962 CLAIMING THE RANCHER'S HEART—Cindy Kirk

Footloose Stacie Collins had a knack for matchmaking. After inheriting her grandma's home in Montana, she and two gal pals decided to head for the hills and test their theories of love on the locals. When their "scientific" survey yielded Josh Collins as Stacie's ideal beau, it must have been a computer error—or was this rugged rancher really a perfect match?

SSECNMBPA0209